Two Much

KARA KEEN

Acknowledgements

Thanks to Scott for being my biggest cheerleader and to Faith Freewoman who is way more than an editor. Kudos to family and friends who listen to me talking about my characters and probably think I'm crazy but smile anyway.

To all of you out there who love reading romance—thanks for your support and words of praise!

Chapter One

Anne

SOMETIMES I WANT to be nice. I mean, *nice*, like my sister. She always notices the lady with the baby who's struggling to get through the door, and runs back to swing the door wide, ushering the nice lady, her draggy-foot toddler, and her baby into the building. The nice girl helps the nice lady. I wish I noticed these opportunities but I just don't.

Rainbow Brite, that's what I call my sister Ariana, but she hates that nickname 'cause it makes her sound like an airhead. When I first started calling her that, I only meant that she was impossibly optimistic. On the other end of her rainbow is her intense sexuality, this aura that follows her around, dragging men into her orbit. It's as if our natures were preordained the day we were born, when my sister got the sexy name and I got the plain one—Anne. I mean, she's my twin, and we look alike, but I would rather read a book than have sex. I just don't get it, what the fuss is about.

And believe me, there's plenty of fuss. Every man we meet has the same fantasy—'Maybe this time I'll live my wildest jerk-off dream and be in the middle of these identical girls.' Some of them are speechless while they imagine it, tongue-tied by visions of one girl doing *this* and the other doing *that*. You know. Others carry on a polite conversation but you can see the fantasy forming in their minds, their eyes raking you over so they can fill in the details later. They get this glazed look in their eyes and the smile gets bigger and bigger, so big they have to lick their lips. If it wasn't so stupid, it would be funny—men who are normally intelligent and disciplined suddenly turning into slobbering wolves. I'm sick of it.

Sometimes I want to dye my hair and bake in a tanning bed so we don't look alike anymore, so my red hair and pale skin go away. Maybe then someone would see *me,* Anne, the young woman who loves to read and listen to music, instead of Anne-who-is-half-of-my-identical-twin-fantasy.

But you know I'll never do it, the hair dyeing and skin baking. I'm realistic about my looks. You have to be that way when you're a redhead because you're just...well...different. You're a minority. It starts in second or third grade, when they make fun of you because of your pale skin and your freckles. You know the nicknames...carrot top, freckle face, ketchup, copper top, Irish, Ginger, Lucy, Chucky.

One guy I dated thought red hair was just weird and told me to dye my hair brown. Obviously it was only that one date.

Recently Ariana and I finally figured out the whole hair and makeup thing, and we've optimized our hair and blue eyes with just the right shades of lipstick, foundation, etc. We're curvy-ish, but luckily we both like to work out and keep the hourglass from becoming a jelly jar.

Regarding the twin fantasy, though, apparently I'm an enabler. That's what the shrink said. My sister suggested I talk to this shrink because I'm twenty-two and I'm a virgin. That's right, I've never had sex. And this is a problem, why?

"Because you're afraid," say my sister and my shrink. No mystery there, of course. I had a boyfriend for six months my freshman year in college. Wyatt was two years older, and he said he was "being patient with me" because we hadn't had sex yet, and then things ended...badly.

There may be truth to that, and truth to the idea that I've enabled my dependent relationship with my sister. By allowing myself to be dragged around in Ariana's trajectory, I've been pulled into a life of passive twinship. Now we've legitimized the whole dysfunctional relationship by becoming business partners in a new online store, Two Much.

And what do we sell on Two Much? No, not high fashion handbags, shoes, cosmetics, or costume jewelry. That would make sense. No, we sell sex toys and sexy clothing, the classy kind that normally arrive at your house wrapped in plain brown paper. But ours arrive wrapped in elegant, creamy, off-white paper embossed with a pattern of French fleur-de-lis. That was actually my idea, making it look like our products are a box of elegant chocolates, ready to pop into your mouth.

Ugh, did I just say that, "ready to pop into your mouth"? The nature of our business has made the whole problem with the identical twin fantasy much, much worse, and yet...let's be honest. It helps sell sex toys. The recording of me and Ariana on *The Meredith Vieira Show* plays in a never-ending loop on our YouTube channel and our website, creating unending links to the wide web world, and selling scads of vibrators and black, shiny lingerie. She talked to us about being young entrepreneurs, role models for other young women, while the three of us kind of danced around the sex toy issue, making humorous comments about boxes and batteries but never being *specific*, if you know what I mean.

When we first put the clip from the *Vieira* show up on our cover page, so many people were watching it that the site crashed and we lost a ton of sales. "Why would that happen? What's so interesting about it?" I asked Owen. Owen is the guy who runs our warehouse and oversees our social media, reaching out on Twitter, Pinterest, Instagram and Facebook to lead people to the website. Ariana and I wonder why he has this part-time, low-paying job with us, since he has a degree and he does fabulous, super-techie things without breaking a sweat. But we're afraid to lose him, so it's a don't-ask, don't-tell situation.

That day he blushed completely red and turned away, clearing his throat. "I'll...uh...have to figure that out." I know nothing about him, except that he does a great job for us, but I swear he might be even shyer than I am. Really hot, and kind of handsome in a geeky kind of way, but he doesn't say much.

The minute he headed for the door at the speed of light, I knew. "It's the goddamn twin fantasy, isn't it? A zillion dudes are watching us and jerking off, that's why the site crashed, isn't it?! Goddamn it!" I slapped my hand down, flat, the loud bang making him flinch.

Owen stopped, his hand on the doorknob. He knew I was upset, because I don't usually swear. Without turning around, he said, "Uh, yeah. That's probably true, though I wish it wasn't. I'm trying to fix it, and I will." He turned to look me in the eye, trying to reassure me, I guess. "I'll have it back up by the end of the day."

I'm sorry, that was hi-larious! Who but a saint could let that go? I almost shot snot out of my nose when I started laughing, unable to control myself. Owen's face turned scarlet when he realized his serious 'get it back up' comment had backfired. (Backfired—see? When you start down this road, the puns only get worse!) He left without further comment. I had to hand it to him, though. I wasn't angry anymore, just laughing my ass off, and thinking how seriously cute he looks when he blushes.

Owen kept his promise, and the clip was back up on the

website and out into the world by the end of the day. His desk was out in the open, up against a grey wall in the warehouse that I had to pass on the way to my car. "Hey, I saw, you did a great job," I said, careful not to repeat the "get it up" thing out loud. And keep a straight face.

He stood, towering over me, and took off his glasses. Though he was totally in my space, I didn't mind. In fact, I found myself hoping he'd move closer. I'd never noticed those green eyes before, or the muscular arms bulging out of his T-shirt. And what about that bit of tattoo peeking out? He didn't blush this time when he said, "I did a major upgrade. There won't be any more problems keeping the site up. It'll be up forever if you want it to be."

I felt a rush of excitement, and now *I* was blushing. "Uh, thanks. Great job," I said in a pathetically feeble whisper. I didn't realize I was holding my breath until I got in my car.

Chapter Two

Ariana

THERE ARE TWO kinds of guys. The first is the kind you can actually have. They take you wherever you want to go, and urge you to order the lobster, as if paying for your lobster will move them up on the scale of desirability. But the mere fact that you can easily have them, no strings, is the reason you don't want them. And they've got nuthin' to say about it, 'cause the reason they want *you* is because they can't have you. Screwed up, right?

Then there's the other kind of guy, the kind you can't have. He's the guy you think about when you hear that song on the radio, the song that goes on and on about why, why, why?! Because you don't know why you want this guy so badly, you just know you do.

Sanjay was the second type. We met freshman year, when Anne and I moved into the freshman dorm, and he saw my mother struggling with a heavy box of whatever. Swooping in with a big smile, he took the box from her. "Let me get that for you, ma'am," he said, tucking the box under one arm, grabbing my laundry basket, and striding confidently through the dorm's front door while the three of us waddled along behind, weighed down by our giant bags of color-coordinated linens. We were faced with an intimidating line of similarly-burdened family groups at the elevator. "The stairs are right over here," he gestured, with a jerk of his head.

"But we're on the fourth floor!" said Anne.

"You three stay here, I'll make a few trips, then we'll take the last bit up in the elevator together. Sound good?" His smile was dazzling, and my mom was quite taken with his English accent. Let's face it, we all were. What followed for me was a great eighteen months of fabulous sex and epic parties at Sanjay's fraternity house.

"Ariana I love you," he would say. "I can't live without you, can you imagine what our kids will look like? We'll be incredible together." He gave me a printed Chatbook of special times we shared, and surprised me with a necklace with my favorite Peter Pan quote: "Second star to the right and straight on 'til morning." When I thought back to those times, the images washed over me, circling my consciousness, still creating a terrible craving in my soul.

And the whole time, the whole fucking time, he was seeing another girl. Not just seeing her, he was engaged to her! Believe it or not, I saw photos of their engagement party in Bandra (near Mumbai) on Facebook. By friending a friend of a friend of Sanjay's, I took a little cultural excursion into the world of Sanjay the Deceiver. She's a very pretty girl, and he looked so fucking *happy* in the pics, just like he looks in photos with me. I thought about worming my way through to her Facebook page and sending her some of "our" lovey shots, but...I'm just not that much of a bitch. My brother Cole's girlfriend Tania has a saying I like, "Don't make enemies for free," which in this case would mean "don't break her heart, there's nothing in it for you."

How could he, how could he, HOW COULD HE??!! How could he touch me so tenderly, how could he make love to me and teach me to make love to him, praising everything about my body, kissing every inch of me? He was the best kind of lover, exploring and touching, making me feel so alive! And I knew his body the way he knew mine, I knew the sounds he made when he was ready to come, when he was inside me, when it felt so good, but neither one of us was ready to come yet.

I should have gotten the hint when his parents came to town and he didn't introduce us. "They're very traditional, and I haven't told them about us yet." Well, yeah, because you're engaged, and when you go home on school holidays, you're with her!

I had a dream about Sanjay where he was making love to me, but when I turned around it was his fiancée's face. I woke up crying, hiccupping and gasping for air after swimming up to a light I saw on the surface of reality. I guess that means his lies were so cynical and calculating it took my breath away.

Chapter Three

Anne

MY SISTER AND I were in the lobby of a showroom at the Boca Casino, attending the premiere of *Romancing Vegas*, a new show produced by friends of our older twin brothers, Cole and Jack. We went "full twin" for the evening, wearing identical sexy dresses in different colors.

I like to think Oksana, the genius behind this sexy cirque-ish burlesque show, is a friend of *ours* now, too, along with Oksana's boyfriend, the famous MMA fighter named Primo. We met Primo and Oksana on Thanksgiving, along with Oksana's sister, Tania, the woman Cole is dating. They seemed to have lots of adventures while they and a bunch of new friends pitched in to help Oksana develop the show over the past few months.

Of course, we're just "the little sisters," but Oksana trusted us to live-tweet about the show. Pretty cool, and the champagne was free. That night, though, Ariana looked a little starstruck. "Hey, Rainbow Brite! You have that Santa look on your face," I said, looking closely at her.

"No. What?" Ariana asked, knowing full well exactly what I was referring to.

"You know, that look you got when Mom took us to see Santa, and you got all happy and sparkly and I cried because I was scared of his freaky facial hair?" It was an annual thing back then...we have the hilarious pictures to prove it. Even I, the crybaby, had to admit the sight of identical red-haired girls on Santa's knees, one horrified and one smiling, is funny.

Ariana leaned back, propping her elbows on the bar, a pose that not only highlights her boobs, but also makes her look confident, like she doesn't give a shit what anybody thinks. Which is natural for her, because she doesn't. I turned, trying to look indifferent while I checked out the ridiculously hot guy who was putting that dreamy look on her face. Aaaand...wow, there he was. Tall and muscular, of course. A total badass with piercing blue eyes, shiny black hair that was longer on top, and James Bond-level tuxedo. Not my type, but his confident posture and cocky stare in our direction marked him as a member of Ariana's perfect species—a serial seducer in a dark suit.

"He's standing next to Jack, so it looks like they're friends," Ariana said. Her face was a little flushed, her voice breathy. Jeez, so much for looking like she didn't give a shit!

"Well, duh, I figured that out. He's the tall guy, longish hair, who doesn't look, uh, domesticated. I can totally see him being friends with Jack." Though elegantly dressed, he looked... *dangerous*, like he drives fast and lives faster than everybody else. Which is just like our brother Jack, but this hottie was younger...late 20's I'd say. I squinted at Ariana.

Her eyes were locked in on *him*. "I know, right?"

That's the reply she gives when she is absolutely not listening. I tried again. "I *said*...oh, forget it. You're mesmerized." I touched her arm, and she flinched, rolling her eyes at me. "We're supposed to be hanging out with the family, so I say go over there and introduce yourself. Even if you just stand there looking horny, like you are right now, Jack will introduce you."

She sucked in a breath and took my hand. "Come with me? We can do our twin thing, and I get to meet my latest mistake."

I owed her this one. People in general, and men in particular, are usually so amazed at our resemblance that we have a laugh about it. It starts with a normal glance, then they see the twin, then the eyeballs click back, like *"Hey, is that the same girl? Did she suddenly move?"* It's a great icebreaker. Ariana did the twin team thing for me, helping me interview Owen (I'd already started crushing on him) for the job at our warehouse. I took her hand and squeezed. "Okay, sis, let's do this."

Jack saved the day, holding out his arm and hugging each of us when we walked up, his other arm in a sling (long story I won't get into here).

"Heeey, ladies, you look so pretty tonight. This is Daniella's brother, Javier. I met him on Thanksgiving," he said, giving us each a kiss on the forehead while he turned us toward Mr. Dark and Handsome. "Javier, these are the *other* Carleton twins, my sisters Ariana and Anne." When Javier smiled and shook our hands, Jack quipped, "As you can see, they got the looks in the family."

To his credit, Javier shook my hand as warmly as he did my sister's, but he held onto hers just a liiiitle bit longer, you know what I mean? Which was totally appropriate, considering the sparks flying between those two.

"Jack," he said, "you're a humble guy, but in this case you're absolutely right." His smile was setting Ariana's pants on fire, I could tell because she was at a loss for words, which *never* happens. "You guys are tweeting about the show tonight, did I hear that right?"

Ariana nodded, opening her mouth to say something but nothing came out. Believe me when I say *that* was a total first. "Yeah," I jumped in, "I downloaded an app on her phone so we can post on #RomancingVegas, but..." I held out the phone, "...you're supposed to be able to live-stream videos too, but how?"

Jack shrugged but Javier grabbed it, raising one of those fierce black eyebrows at me. "Have you thought about maybe alternating, one of you tweeting photos while the other shoots video?" His confident tone conveyed the idea that we definitely *should* think about it...and I agreed.

"Great idea! Give Ariana some tips on the app, and I'll do the rest." He took her aside, speaking in this low, sexy voice and smiling the whole time. Gliding along next to him, Ariana appeared to be caught in a tractor beam, unable to disengage from his miles of white teeth. I grabbed my brother and whispered "Holy cow, Jack, have you seen Ariana at a loss for words before? Ever?"

Squinting in their direction, Jack looked wary. "I don't know him that well, but Javier seems like, you know...kind of a player."

"So...good-looking and charming? Like you, you mean?" We both laughed, punching each other in the arm like little kids. Jack and Cole are so much older than we are, it sometimes feels like they're uncles instead of brothers, but they care a lot and make the effort to stay in touch.

Jack put his arm around me and squeezed. "I heard your old boyfriend Wyatt was out of jail. Any problems Annie-girl?"

I shivered at the mention of that idiot's name and kissed Jack on the cheek. "Haven't heard a peep out of him. Thanks for asking." I took another sip of champagne, hopefully washing the sour taste of Wyatt out of my mouth.

Since I was just twenty-two, it still felt weird to be legally drinking a glass of champagne around my family, so I attempted to keep the giggling to a minimum. "But getting back to Ariana, Jack. She's usually the one in charge with men so...why, do you know something bad about Javier?"

"We took a spin in the Porsche I rented on Thanksgiving, and he gave it a workout. I think my face flattened out when we went zero to ninety in about four seconds. Uh...kidding. But not." He tilted his head back, remembering. "Anywaaaay, good points. He, uh, loves his sisters. Pretty good at carving a turkey. Owns his own really cool business selling restored Volkswagens. That's all I know. Seriously, though, do you think we should be worried about her? I mean, her with him, if this goes somewhere?" Then he revealed what he was truly worried about. "Will it be weird if I'm with Javier's sister Daniella and Javier is with my sister?"

Now *I* was worried. I'd facilitated the intro, so this was suddenly my responsibility. "I'll keep an eye on it. And no, it won't be weird. It happens all the time. Remember that Mom's sister Diane dated Dad's brother Joe back in the day?"

He thought for a minute. "I remember that Joe was such a prick that Aunt Diane still isn't speaking to Dad. So that didn't end well."

I hadn't heard that story. "Uh...oh. There is potential there, sure, good and evil, family and foe, yada yada."

Looking over at Ariana, I noticed she'd not only regained her conversational skills but she was touching him while they talked, a flirty tap on the hand, a clasp of the forearm. "But I think it's too late, she's putting the moves on him already."

It seemed to me this would be another step in my sister's sexual journey, the usual titanic struggle between equally strong, independent people who enjoy the heat when they set

each other on fire. I might not have even *started* my sexual
journey yet, but watching them made me long to make some
sparks fly with Owen.

Javier

I knew I was a goner the minute Ariana touched me. Before
that, I knew she was younger, and that she was Jack's sister,
and therefore kryptonite. You can never have a casual
relationship with your sister's boyfriend's sister. It will
automatically escalate to something serious, a topic of much
discussion by both families involved.

I knew all this, and yet the minute I saw her, I started
willing her to look at me, hurling the flames in my gut across
the room to get her attention. I took my time staring at the
forbidden fruit, those two beautiful sisters, their long, shapely
legs and curvy bodies leaning against the bar. And the long
red hair, dear God!

I knew who they were immediately, because Daniella told
me about the identical sisters and how different they actually
were from each other, one a wild child and the other
conservative and sweet. Miss Wild Child identified herself,
turning and putting her elbows behind her on the bar. She
wore a purple dress that pulled at her curvy places and
screamed SEXY...to me and every other man lounging
around the lobby, checking her out.

Thank God, before she looked at me Jack came over and
gave me a warm handshake, and we spent a few minutes
catching up. That made it easy to get my game on, meet the
sisters and, without bothering to ask myself why, volunteer

some tips for Ariana's upcoming tweet-fest, thereby separating her from her siblings.

"So this is how you can publish the link to Twitter..." I was talking quietly and leaning in so she was close, so close I could feel her warmth. As soon as I opened my mouth, I realized she probably already knew how to do this but she made no attempt to step away while I walked her through how to check the stream during the performance. "You can check on people who're retweeting and live-blogging, and jump back to taking pictures. Here, watch," I murmured, and she gave me a sexy pout when I focused on her lips.

Holding it out for a selfie, I pulled her in tight, first touching my cheek to hers and then snapping another one while I kissed her cheek. I was glad we'd wandered into the hall, because the heat between us built fast, especially when I imagined putting some love bites onto that pale neck of hers. A flush spread from her cleavage to her neck to her face, highlighting the cute freckles I hadn't noticed before. Grinning, she let me stare, her head tipping back to give me a better look. "See?" I said. "Our first kiss, and I've recorded the historic moment. Let's see how we look."

A little flustered and off-balance, she sputtered "You...you're too smooth, you're making my head spin." I liked her reaction, honest, and not trying to be cool. When she leaned in again to look at the pictures, I could smell her spicy perfume.

I turned away from her after I showed her the three shots (and sent them to my phone), and said "Let's see what's in your gallery here, Miss Carleton."

She lunged for the phone, but I just put my arm tight around her, holding her arms to her sides, wishing the hips wiggling into my side were naked and circling...well, you know. I clicked through her photos while she squealed and we both laughed. "Oh, look at this, Ariana with drunk eyes holding a pink cocktail. Hmmm, nice, here's the part of your tattoo that's hiding under your gown right now. Who took that picture? And here you are playing soccer with your sister." I looked down at her. "You play soccer?"

"We both do. We're good, so good we organized a coed soccer league." She stuck her chin out, challenging me. "Wanna play, big man?"

"Yes. Yes, I do." I licked my lips. "But you want me on *your* team, believe me. Remember, my people are from Mexico, we're genetically programmed to play soccer."

"Okay. You're on my team, Tuesday night. SNU field #4, behind the Rec Center." There was a flash of hunger in those eyes of hers, but no hesitation, and she whispered in my ear. "Better have your game face on, Tuxedo Boy!" She walked toward her family surprisingly quickly, considering the height of those killer heels, giving me a little wave over her shoulder.

I sent myself a text with the soccer details and a reminder to increase my cardio for the next four days and look for my cleats. My bravado was totally fake, and there was definite potential for the young 'uns to embarrass me unless...maybe Jack and Cole would be there, and they're even older than I am.

My resolution to stay away from Jack's sister was weakening by the minute, aided by the sway of her hips while she walked away. This weird compulsion to tattoo her body with the word *mine* overtook me and my jaw was clenched so tightly it hurt. Buuut... I'd promised my mom to care for my baby brother in the back of the theater while she sat in the audience and watched Daniella in the show. After catching a rehearsal last week, I could follow along while swinging the sleeping little dude around, thinking about Ariana's lips and her cleavage and, weirdly, her freckles. Hot.

Yeah, she was quiet at first, a little shy when I complimented her, but my relentless flirting didn't faze her. Kind of the opposite, which I found intriguing. She was hot, funny...different, this one, and I knew I was going to have to work for it for a change. She was young, she was Jack's sister, and she seemed like a nice person, all reasons she could never be on my usual hit-em-and-quit-em list.

Still, I found myself strategizing about how to impress her on Tuesday night. *Oh, hell, yeah, I'm in trouble.*

Ariana

Javier had me the moment he took that baby in his arms and actually knew what to do. Rocking and cooing, Javier didn't know I was watching when his mother handed him an infant (his brother, half-brother?) so she could sit up front and watch her daughter, his sister Daniella, dance in the show. I'd gone to the bathroom and saw the handoff on my way back to my seat.

Picture it for me, will you? Could *you* resist a hot guy in a tuxedo, soothing a sleeping baby in the back of a theater so Mom could relax and watch Sis do her thing?

I swear, I felt my ovaries heat up and scream, "Him, he's the father of your children!" (And at twenty-two, I hadn't even thought about having children yet.) When he looked up and saw me watching him, he didn't miss a beat, giving me the eyebrows and the quick nod that said "Business as usual, piece of cake, wanna give it a shot?"

I shook my head and held up my phone while the orchestra tuned up in the background, reminding him that Anne and I were supposed to live-tweet the entire show. He shrugged and smiled, gesturing for me to go ahead and sit down. Was it significant that we'd only known each other for twenty minutes and we could already talk in gestures?

I started down the aisle, but glanced back just when Javier lifted that sweet child to his lips and kissed his forehead. It was the kind of kiss you give when you want to deeply inhale the delicious baby smell. My heart squeezed, kind of like a heart attack, but in a good way. Whoo-boy, sometimes you don't know what you want until you see it.

The show was amazing, moving swiftly from Oksana's aerial dance to Daniella's super-sexy tour through "The History of Booty." Ninety minutes flew by, with erotic circus acts involving what had to be some of the best-looking people on earth, and ending with a Ukrainian dancer/ juggler for whom gravity was apparently optional. It was easy to represent the show in our tweets, because the visuals were stunning and the show was just sooo freakin' *cool!* We were incredibly proud of Tania and our brothers for helping out with this phenomenal show, and we screamed like the rest of the crowd when Oksana thanked them and had them stand and take a bow at the end. Nobody had ever seen anything like *Romancing Vegas*, and the audience leaped to their feet at the end, hooting, hollering, and applauding for, like, ten minutes.

Beautiful Oksana stood there, wrapped in her red silk costume under a gorgeous chandelier, bowing and hugging everyone in the cast and throwing kisses. When Ed Sheeran's romantic song *Thinking Out Loud* came on, we sat down, thinking there was going to be some kind of encore.

Instead, Oksana's boyfriend, Primo, stood in the aisle, right there next to us in the tenth row. He held a big bunch of roses and said the sweetest, most passionate things to Oksana. Wearing a microphone so we could hear, he talked about how she inspired him and changed his life, and then he asked her to marry him! Of course, she said yes. He jumped up onto the stage and kissed her, and I could see the big ol' rock he put on her finger all the way back in the tenth row!

Anne and I were passing a tissue back and forth, crying at this crazy romantic spectacle and, of course, hoping for that kind of love in our own lives someday. I was remembering Sanjay, of course, and Anne was probably sad about her prick of an ex-boyfriend, goddamn abuser-dude Wyatt. Both those guys were like open wounds, very hard to heal. I wondered what Javier, ladies' man extraordinaire, thought of the whole proposal thing. It seemed like it would be his worst nightmare, but when we stumbled out of the theater, wiping the mascara from under our eyes, he and the rest of the Flores gang were gone. Sigh. The weight of his attention was a narcotic, and I was already hooked, already letting him creep into my thoughts.

I was already waiting for his first text, dammit.

Chapter Four

Anne

"I'M SURPRISED YOU didn't go to the meeting. You could've done your twin thing on them." Owen said, leaning against the picnic table behind our office on Monday, his arms crossed, sexy muscles popping out of a *Big Bang Theory* T-shirt that says *Bazinga!* It's one of the things I like about him, he totally embraces his inner nerd while also being a master of the one-armed pushup. We love having him in our Tuesday night soccer league, Sin City Coed Soccer, because he's super-fit.

"I had an exam this morning, but I'm at the meeting in spirit," I said. "I create fierce PowerPoints, and the one I put on Ariana's laptop last night was my masterpiece."

Owen knew Ariana was at a big hotel on the strip right now, meeting with a potential supplier, using my PowerPoint to convince those people our little site was worth their time. "I'm the boring sister, the nice, steady girl who hides behind the spread sheets. I get too nervous and clam up at meetings. Ariana is the one who's out there pushing the limits, making people pay attention to our company." Nodding and frowning, Owen was listening closely. He put some papers on my desk and got us each an iced tea from the office fridge.

"Why is that hiding?" Owen appeared to be insulted on my behalf. "Taking care of the financials and the other back end stuff while you finish your degree isn't hiding. I can't believe you think that about yourself. What does that make me? I schlep boxes around, prepare shipping, and keep the online stuff going. Am I hiding?"

I literally had to close my mouth and sit on my hands at his choice of words. Ariana and I had discussed his underemployed status ad nauseum. *Yes, you are hiding. Something.* "That makes you a godsend! Owen, you have made this whole thing possible. You're so professional and you're so...you." I faltered, struggling to put his other qualities into words.

His eyebrows quirked with interest, and he had a twinkle in his eyes when he leaned over the table, covering my hand with his. "What does that mean, Annie-girl? How am I so me?"

I froze. My friend Taylor's mom and my brothers call me Annie. Is that how he thinks of me, as a little girl? But it didn't feel that way, it wasn't said that way. The nickname and his touch seemed so affectionate I was tongue-tied, but after a few fluttering-heart moments, I collected my thoughts.

"You're the person who came in here and turned our crazy marketing project into a real business, don't you remember? In a matter of a week, you put those first ten products up on the site and had the PayPal and the credit card stuff going. You gave us a list of the other decisions we had to make, and copy we had to write, and—bada-boom!—we were rolling. You're so...you're such a good person and so smart."

That cued his crooked smile, and he squeezed my hand, but I managed to add "We don't deserve you."

He shook his head, and I put my hand over his and hesitated, struggling to form the real question. "We really *don't* deserve you, Owen. We know that. You could be running your own company, a big company." He stood up straighter, taking his hand away and pursing his lips, but I couldn't stop asking this now I'd started. "You have to admit that you're kind of…underemployed, working here for us part-time, right?"

He finished up his iced tea, avoiding my eyes. "I do have some other responsibilities, personal responsibilities that take a lot of time." Tension radiated from that hot body of his, and my pulse thumped in my ears. Did the way he said "personal" mean he didn't want to answer questions about it, or was that just me?

Yes, we've noticed how you sometimes get a phone call and leave the office suddenly at breakneck speed. And how you look at your phone when we're hanging out in the bar after soccer. Was he married and had a kid, did he have another job, was he on probation? I thought these things, but his manner warned me not to ask them out loud.

I paused; he was stonewalling me. I changed tactics. "I mean, the day we interviewed you, we were two college kids who hadn't even rented an office yet. What made you decide to come work for us?"

He stood, leaning forward, and tucking a lock of hair behind my ear. "It was you, Annie. I wanted to come work for you." He started cleaning up the picnic table. Clearing his throat, he added "I…uh…guess we should get back to work?" The man possesses the gift of making an exit well before you actually *want* him to leave.

Lately when he walked away from me, I kind of immediately missed him. The absence of his face, his voice, his focus on me…it left a void I hated living in. He wasn't a big texter, either, but then neither was I. And what would we text about? We do talk about everything and nothing, TV shows and music along with work stuff, but I couldn't see him sending me a flirty text. When I was at my morning classes, I couldn't wait to get to the office.

It occurred to me while I shuffled back inside that all this wanting probably wasn't going to end well.

Owen

People say I'm a man of few words, so here's my few words about Anne. I like her. She's smart and funny, and when she walks into a room, she brings the sunshine with her, just makes everything seem like the first day of spring. Corny, right?

I was attracted to her the minute I heard her voice because, of course, when I first met the sisters I was kind of thrown off by the twin thing. It's kind of...uncomfortable, you don't know where to look first without being rude, while your eyes go back and forth from one to the other. It's like your brain is saying "Wait a minute, are they really that identical?" But then Anne laughed. That laugh of hers made everyone—not just me—feel like she was their new best friend.

The other night at the bar after soccer, she sat close to me and told me funny stories about the people in that league of theirs. She's so sharp about people and how they tick, I haven't laughed that much in a while. Because the music was so loud, we were leaning into each other and both feeling...attraction. It hit me right where it counts, and I could tell from the flush on her cheeks and the way her voice was kind of husky she was feeling it too. When she got up to go to the restroom, I got a prime view of her gorgeous butt while she slid past me.

A blonde in a sexy outfit, not from the soccer league, sat down next to me and started chatting me up. Anne saw her and stopped to talk to some people she knew, glancing over every once in a while to see how I was handling it. Truth be told, all I could think about was Anne, and I got rid of blondie as politely as I could.

I couldn't get the pornographic images of Anne out of my head, and I had an honest talk with myself while she was flitting around the bar talking with others from the league. I kept thinking about the freckles on her nose, wondering where else they were on her body. I thought I was just the guy to do a detailed search to find that out. I took this job because I liked her right away. She doesn't have a boyfriend. My life has some complications, but she seems to have some bullshit to deal with too. I was finally ready to see where this would go.

My opportunity presented itself right away. Someone sat in her seat on my left, so when she came back I patted my legs. "Why don't you sit here, on my lap?" She hesitated for a second and then sat down, hooking her arm around my shoulders. Our faces were now about a foot apart, and I could feel the side of her breast pressing against my chest. I wondered if she could feel how aroused I was getting, and then thought *I'm fine with her knowing how aroused I'm getting*. I figured I'd gotten this started, and I wasn't going to talk myself out of it.

"Should we...uh...is this a good idea?" she whispered, her voice trembling. We were both aware of the surge of heat between us, which had been building for a while now.

"I think it's a great idea." Her giggle shook both of us, and I was grinning like a fool.

We continued the conversation we started earlier, talking and laughing for a while, but conscious of our bodies touching. Her cheeks were burning, but she managed to tell me a story about a girl in one of her classes who said her mother had a vasectomy and another about a couple who made out in the back of her history class. The professor called them out on it and commented, "I'm flattered, I didn't know my lecture was that sexy."

"I kind of envy people who are that spontaneous, don't you? I'd like to make out with you right now."

"Owen, what? No!"

"I'll try not to take that personally," I laughed. My phone sounded off, and I checked it. "Damn," I said, "I have to go." Pulling her in close with my arm across her back, I asked "If you won't make out with me, can I at least kiss you good night?"

"Owen…" she giggled, pushing me away a little. I kissed her, and she stopped pushing and kissed me back. It was just on the lips, but it was hot anyway, I guess because it was her. It felt so good, like every kiss before this prepared me for this one. She seemed a little dazed when I lifted her off my lap, turned, and kissed her forehead when I set her down on my seat.

"See you at the office," I said. Expecting her to fling a funny line at me, I was surprised to see her give me kind of a limp-wristed wave. I must be better at flirting than I thought I was, because Anne Carleton was speechless.

Chapter Five

Ariana

MY SISTER AND I started the Sin City Coed Soccer League our freshman year, and we had some odd rules. Eight people on each team, equal number of men and women. Twenty-minute halves with a thirty-minute halftime break for socializing. (Socializing—that was the whole point, right?)

Javier showed up looking like a Latino David Beckham, of course, wearing shorts that highlighted those massive quads of his, with tribal tattoos peeking out of his soccer shirt. Taylor saw him and whistled under her breath. "You said he was hot, but damn! *Big* trouble!"

"Well, you know, the bigger they are the harder they fall," I said, letting him hear me when he walked up.

"Luckily I don't have to fall tonight, because I'm on your team, right?" he said, giving me a kiss on the cheek with a cocky smile.

He turned out to be a fantastic player, deflecting the ball to me in the first half after stealing it from the other team. I made a quick run up center, passed the ball to Owen, and he slid a goal in. Later, Javier backpedaled with the ball, cut right, and took a long, forceful strike from thirty yards that whizzed right past their goalie. Taylor slapped him on the back and announced that he could be the new lifetime team member if he wanted to. I shot her a look; that invite might have been a bit premature. What if he turned out to be an asshole?

Anne, me, and our closest girlfriend, Taylor, always play on the same team in the league. Yes, it's strange that my sister and I have the same best friend, even though we have such different personalities. Taylor has always been there for both of us, beginning way back in the day when Taylor's mom became our babysitter. From that day forward, we were the gang of three.

Anne is the quiet one, but she's also the fierce one of us. When we need a hit man, someone to tell somebody off, Taylor and I just get out of her way. When we were seven, a kid named Frank Rago told Taylor to fuck off when we were playing on the playground. She wasn't sure exactly what it meant but when he pushed her off the monkey bars, Taylor told *him* to fuck off. The problem was, a teacher overheard her, and she got detention, and they sent home a note to her mom.

A few days later, Anne sneaked up on Frank Rago and kicked him in the ass. When he turned around to come after her, she head-butted him, leaving a big, red bump in the middle of his forehead! (Hers, too.) He stayed far away from us after that.

The current target of Anne's hostility was Sanjay, and she skulked restlessly around his end of the field during halftime. "C'mon Anne, forget him. Let me buy you a margarita," Taylor said. Rita's Margaritas food truck always visited our games during halftime, and Taylor was trying to drag Anne over there. Owen and Javier followed along for a while, probably wondering what Anne was up to.

"That's Ariana's old boyfriend, Sanjay," Taylor whispered. While they watched, Sanjay was burying his tongue in his latest girlfriend's mouth, making a show of how into each other they were. "When we had a little too much to drink," Taylor said, "we would fantasize about telling his girlfriends he was engaged to a girl back in India, but he didn't keep them around long enough for us to care."

"We wish we could just never see Sanjay again," I added, "but we have the same friends, so we just let it ride."

Our team huddled up before the second half and decided to do some short, sharp passes, and keep the ball tight between us. That idea went up in smoke when Sanjay's team went to an aerial game, heading the ball hard and driving it right past us. Javier used his height to make the best of a bad situation, and ended up falling on the ball, then rolling off just in time for Owen to dribble it away and pass it to me so I could slot it past the goalie. Sanjay didn't look too happy while he watched Javier pick me up on his shoulders and do a victory lap around the field.

Never thinking it was Anne's car, we heard a car alarm in the parking lot and sauntered over there after the game. But it *was* her car. Campus police got there about the same time we did. Owen and Javier got all macho and protective, telling us to stay back while they checked the situation out. Of course we ignored them, getting pissed about the dent in the trunk where it had been pried open. The contents of Anne's purse were scattered all over the trunk. Thank God, I'd left my purse home, 'cause she was driving.

After Anne turned the alarm off, the police motioned us over for a closer look. "Is this your purse, ma'am?" Anne nodded and picked up her phone and wallet. "Would you look it over and tell us if anything's missing?"

After putting things back in one by one and then searching

through her wallet, Anne told them only the cash was missing. "Don't you think it's weird that they didn't take my credit cards or my phone?" she asked. The officer shrugged and handed her a clipboard with paperwork to fill out. We were still able to close the trunk, so that was good.

"See you over at Sparky's?" I said to Javier. That's the bar we always went to after soccer.

"Absolutely." He winked at Anne. "You're okay, right?" She nodded.

I stood right next to Anne because I could see she was shook up. "You need to go home, kid?" I asked her.

She shook her head. "No, no. Don't worry about it."

We both knew she got spooked by these kinds of situations, because of what happened freshman year.

Owen asked if he could ride with us; he could see Anne was upset. "You look like you could use a drink, I'm buying."

She gave me a hug that said she was fine, but I sat behind her, making her laugh on the way to Sparky's. When we walked in, we were greeted by a deafening blast of Black Eyed Peas, and went to the usual bunch of tables reserved for the league. Before long, she was her usual laughing, joking self, sitting very close to Owen and enjoying Javier's stories about finding old Volkswagens on Craigslist.

Javier went to the men's room, and then I noticed him leaning against the jukebox, watching me. The weight of his gaze thrilled me, and I finished up my beer and went over to him.

"Wanna get outta here? Are Anne and Taylor okay?" he asked.

I checked with them, and we were headed out when Jillian, Sanjay's girlfriend, ran her long red fingernails down Javier's arm. Talking to him as if I wasn't there, she crooned, "Heeey! So good to see you again, Javier!"

"Hey, Jillian," he said, barely smiling. "Have you met Ariana? She's one of the founders of the soccer league."

Looking like it was painful to even flick her eyeballs at me, she didn't answer the question but touched his arm again. "I'd love to get together again sometime." Just at that moment, Sanjay showed up and gave Javier the stink eye, dragging Jillian away.

"Do you think she knows Sanjay is engaged?" I said in a loud voice. We swore later we saw Jillian's shoulders stiffen, but we weren't positive.

"Whoa, you go right for the kill, don't you?" Javier handed me a napkin for my tears, I was laughing so hard, and Anne and Taylor, who overheard the whole thing, were convulsing.

Chapter Six

Ariana

WHEN I SAW Javier's car in the parking lot, I pretended to fan myself, as if I was going to faint. "I mean, I know you're in the car business, but this is just…" I rubbed my hands on my shirt before putting them on the car. "Can I touch it all over? I promise I'll be gentle." I petted the sides of his sexy black Karmann Ghia convertible. "What year is it?"

"1969," he said, grinning. When I stroked the curve of the wheel wells and laid my head on the leather convertible top with a sigh, he let loose. His laugh was so musical and genuine, and spontaneous, like a kid's laugh. A playful contrast to his sophisticated style, Javier's unguarded laugh won everyone's heart that night, his very first night at Sin City Coed Soccer, but especially mine.

He lifted me up onto the trunk of the car and stole a hard, fast kiss, holding both my hands while he leaned back, searching my eyes. "Your lust for my car is sexy. Will you be exclusive with it, or are you going to mess around with younger, faster models?"

"Are we still talking about cars here?" I tilted my head, my hands on his shoulders. "'Cause if we aren't, I would describe myself as a serial monogamist, focusing completely on the, uh, car I'm currently driving. How about you?"

I was thrilled with this persona I'd assumed, the sexy girl looking for a good time. I'd had two short relationships in the two years since Sanjay, but "love 'em and leave 'em Ariana" really *sounded* good, didn't she?

"Same," he said, lifting my hands to those hot lips of his. "How 'bout you call your sister and tell her you have a ride? Where am I taking you, Ariana?" Lips just nicely wet, he kissed each of my knuckles, and then turned my hands over and kissed the palms.

Ho. Lee. Shit! Rubber—meet road. This guy gets right to the point. "I'm thinking…your place. Does that work?" Now I pulled our hands toward *my* mouth, squeezing his fingers and putting his thumb in my mouth, sucking it in, then nibbling a little while he slowly slid it out and brushed it against my lower lip.

His eyes were blazing while he slid an arm under my thighs, supporting my back with the other one, and carried me around the car to the passenger side. He opened the door for me when my feet hit the ground, and I sank into the seat. Anne didn't ask any questions when I called her; she saw us leave together.

When he got in and the car started with a roar, he shook his head as we pulled out. "I'm rarely at a loss for words. You got me, girl."

Feeling like the ballsiest bitch in town, I fiddled with the radio and enjoyed the fresh desert breeze while we drove down Tropicana. He kept looking over at me, kind of smirking, while we headed west. "Why are you so surprised?" I asked. "Where did you think I would want to go?"

Laughing again, he looked straight ahead, "I figured, you

know, out to eat, or listen to some music, or whatever."

"Normally, I would probably want to do that but...I don't know. I would just be thinking about how hot you are and how much I want to touch you. Isn't that how guys think?"

Nodding, he reached over and started massaging the back of my neck with one hand. "That's *exactly* how guys think, but I've never met a woman who doesn't want to, uh... drag out the preliminaries, I guess, make the guy jump through a few hoops, you know? Or, hopefully, make sure she feels safe with him." Now he shot me a questioning look.

"I don't know this bold woman in my seat very well, either. Matter of fact I just met her. I'm not shy, but I've never acted like this." Arching into his excellent neck rub, I tried not to purr. "I feel as if I know you and...well, when I saw you rocking your baby brother like that at the theater..." I threw my arms out and said "Beautiful man in a tuxedo kissing a baby's forehead! Jeeeaaackpot!"

He shook with laughter while we headed toward Spring Valley. "You are weird, you know that?"

"You're not the only person to say that. Ask my entire, giant family." We drove along, enjoying the breeze, and I was turning to total mush from his hand on my neck. It didn't feel like he was putting the moves on me, more like he enjoyed touching me. "You give good neck rub, sexy man. I like the calluses on your fingers, they feel good." I kept replaying the moment when I sucked his thumb into my mouth and made love to it. I wasn't sure who that wanton seductress was, but I liked her style.

"The calluses are from working on cars, unfortunately. Those old Volkswagens I buy and sell need work, including this one, and I have guys who do the mechanics, but I get involved in painting and upholstering." He sighed. "There are never enough hands on deck, so I'm right in there with the rest of the guys."

"So...change of subject. When did you date Jillian? And how many Jillians are we going to be meeting around town? Are we talking hundreds? Thousands?"

He scowled, obviously kind of embarrassed. "How do you know I dated her? Maybe I sold her a car."

Chuckling, I shrugged his hand off my neck and attempted to apply the same magic fingers to his neck. "Oh, come on. She gave you that one-who-got-away look, and even said she wants to see you again! What happened?"

He was keeping his eyes on the road, leaning into my neck rub. "The usual. She wanted to move in together, meet my family, and I just didn't feel that way about her."

"And how many times has this happened? I won't hold you to an exact number, just give me a ballpark figure."

His eyes twinkled and he was trying not to laugh. "Are you seriously asking me my number right now?"

"Too soon for that? Okay." Imagining his place as the ultimate bachelor pad, I started wondering out loud about it. "So you have a sixty-inch flat-screen?"

"Check, I have that. Too predictable?"

"Big black leather sectional couch?"

"Check. Are you making fun of me?"

"Kind of. How about a round king-size bed that vibrates and has mirrors on the ceiling?"

"Do you think I'm Austin Powers? He's way cooler than me."

"I agree, and you didn't ask me if we're going to shag, baby."

When he didn't answer, I figured it was time for the next question. "Nothing in the refrigerator but ketchup and beer?"

"No, I have salsa and sriracha too."

When we pulled up to the condo complex, I could see three parking spaces had Flores stenciled on them. "You have roommates?"

"Yes."

I felt deflated and hoped they wouldn't be home. The communal version of the bachelor pad was just not seductive. I pictured a bunch of guys lying around passing a joint, the game perpetually on. "But you have three parking spaces and two are empty, so I guess...will they be home?"

When he came around to open my car door, he was shaking with laughter. I stood and faced him, noticing again how tall he was. "Definitely. You'll like them."

Chapter Seven

Ariana

H E PULLED ME in after him while he keyed in the door, then closed it behind us. We were met by a wall of deafening barking and furry love! Four puggy-looking dogs leaped, twisted and licked with an enthusiasm born of unconditional love. I love dogs, but I stumbled back in surprise, badly twisting my ankle and wincing.

"Damn, I'm sorry," Javier said, but his hands at my waist steadied me, surrounding me with that woodsy scent of his. "I wanted to surprise you. These are my roommates. I rescued them from the shelter." To be heard over the barking, he spoke in a low voice right in my ear while helping me limp toward a chair in the living room. "I had to pick dogs under 35 pounds because of the condo rules. And I bought those other parking spaces for cars I'm working on."

The grey pug jumped on my lap and gave me some nice, wet kisses. It felt so good to hold a dog again (our old dog is buried in the yard), and I scratched behind his ears and his belly at the same time.

"He likes you," Javier said while the dog moaned in ecstasy, his eyes rolling back in his head.

"I read somewhere that the reason they get so excited to smell and lick you comes from the days when they were wolves. They want to see if you brought anything back for them to eat," I said.

When Javier walked toward the couch he was…beaming, I mean grinning from ear to ear, like he was sooo proud. The dogs ran ahead and jumped on the couch, lining up and looking expectantly at Javier. "This is John," he said, leaning in and scratching behind the ears of the black one. The white one sat up on its hind legs. "Paul," he gestured. Paul got a belly rub.

"Wait, don't tell me. George and Ringo are the other ones!" I said, clapping my hands.

"Ringo is actually a girl," he said. "The rest are males."

I wasn't sure which was more adorable, his proud papa display, the fact that they lined up in Beatles' name order, or the dogs themselves. The goofy, affectionate way he filled their dog bowls and let them out the sliding glass door to their poopy pen was melting my heart. My ankle, on the other hand, was expanding, looking a little puffy-looking. I looked around, noticing the soothing teal color on the wall behind the couch, the framed posters of classic Volkswagens, and the area rug. "This does *not* look like a bachelor pad. It's too nice."

Putting some beers from the fridge onto the breakfast bar, he ducked his head, unexpectedly shy. "My mom and Daniella surprised me, fixed it up while I was at work a couple days after Thanksgiving. Before that, it looked…beige." Twisting open the beers, he looked thoughtful. "Besides, it was never an issue. I don't bring women here."

That was surprising. "I feel special," I said. "I guess you trust me not to psycho-stalk you someday."

Javier chuckled at that. "You don't seem like the psycho-stalking type."

When I said someday, we both knew what I meant. The day our relationship was over. Since we'd both been half of an as-yet-unnamed number of couples, it seemed modern to acknowledge that day would come. But sad. Part of me wanted to pretend that day wouldn't come, didn't even exist. Isn't that how it is in romance novels?

When I stood and started limping over, he stared down at my puffy ankle, horrified. "Let me carry you over," he said, and he hiked me up onto his back for a piggyback ride, then plopped me down on a barstool and handed me a beer.

"Better watch it, that's the second time tonight you've picked me up. I'm too heavy, and you'll get a hernia." I always babble like that when I'm nervous. It's my way of getting him to pet me and tell me I'm pretty. And it worked.

He tipped the beer bottle back and sucked down about half of it. "You are not fat. God, please don't be the body-bashing girl. You're gorgeous, you've got that covered, so just get used to me enjoying it. And I like carrying you around, it gives me an excuse to touch you inappropriately."

"Get used to me." I tried not to care, but I liked the sound of that.

"First of all, maybe you don't need an excuse...to touch me, I mean." I felt my face flush at that admission. *Do I sound desperate or confident?* "And second, maybe I'm heavy because of my solid mass of girl-power muscle!" He squeezed my bicep with a chuckle, and then kissed it when I made a muscle for him. "I was a flabby, book-obsessed kid, and now I'm a weight-lifting Amazon."

Shuffling around the kitchen, he smirked. "I had a thing for the editor of my high school newspaper. You remind me of her. But in those days, I waited until a girl talked to *me*, not the other way around."

"I was so clueless in high school, I probably wasn't even aware girls could do that."

"But you've figured it out now."

"I *have* figured it out, and it can be a lot of fun."

When he nuked a circle of brie cheese in the microwave and put out a crusty loaf of bread and grapes, I started laughing. If domestic girl porn is an actual thing, this was it. "Who knew you were, like, Martha Stewart?" Enjoying the food, I looked up at him "I feel like you were always the cool guy in high school, the guy who would never notice me. Do you know what Anne said about you when she saw you in the theater? She said you didn't look domesticated." I heard the hum of texts arriving on the phone in my pocket, but for the first time in ages I wanted to pay attention and stay in this moment.

Javier

I let the dogs in, and she stopped chattering, both of us tearing into the cheese with big hunks of bread, finishing up our beers and having another. Smart and honest by nature, I knew she would analyze everything that was said and done when the evening was over. I wanted to be on the good side of that analysis.

I stood between her legs, looking in her eyes and feeding her grapes one at a time. "You...sound like you're nervous. Am I doing something to make you nervous?" She was giving me clear signals that she wanted to get physical, but I wanted her to take the lead at every step of the way.

"You're doing nothing and everything to make me nervous. Just by...being you." Resting her head on my belly and pulling me in close, her fingers spread on my butt, she took the lead with blunt force honesty. "I need a shower, don't you? Can we shower together?"

I'm pretty sure I looked surprised, and I'm positive I was speechless. So much for the cool guy. I closed a handful of her hair in my fist and when I saw my fingers sifting through that gorgeous red silk, I swear I saw stars. My lips found the pulse hammering in her neck before she pulled me in, grinding into me before I pulled her head back and kissed her. I didn't even attempt to kiss her gently; her shaky moans begged me for rougher, harder, faster. And I was so happy to oblige.

The whole experience was surreal, everything happening so easily, kinda like the first time my girl said yes to me when we were in high school. I explored Ariana's mouth and sucked on her tongue, and she answered me with a low hum of pleasure.

"Here, let's take turns." I whispered. "I take my shirt off and..."

Instead of taking her shirt off, she ran her hands over my chest and licked—fucking *licked*—the barbell piercing on my left nipple with that little pink tongue of hers, sending a shiver straight to my dick. Her eyes looking up at me were naughty. "My God, that piercing is so hot! Am I cheating on my turn? It's just that I..." She stopped abruptly and took off her soccer shirt, pulling the sports bra off as well and throwing them both on the floor.

Freckled and milky white, her skin was exactly like the redhead fantasies I'd been having since I met her, only better. I'd imagined how she'd look naked about twenty times a day, but the reality was...breathtaking. Her breasts were full and tipped up, her nipples larger than I imagined, rosy pink like her lips and the polish on her nails. That color imprinted on my brain, and I don't remember now, but apparently I was just standing there staring. She cleared her throat and chuckled, "First time with a redhead?"

All I could do was nod, and I backed up to the stool she was sitting on, wrapping her legs around my waist so I could carry her to my bathroom. I've never been so affected by the feel of a woman's breasts, the soft, sexy bounce of them against my back, her nipples pebbling up while she kissed my neck, her hands crossed under my chin. Her bare chest against my skin…this must be what heaven feels like. Holy shit, my cock was so fucking *ready*.

When I set her down on the counter, I saw the tattoo on her shoulder blade in the mirror. I circled around, taking in the curve of her spine and her cute little nose and sexy lips. *Damn!* The tattoo was small, the outline of a bird in flight. The unusual part was the color, which exactly matched the deep, fiery color of her hair. I ran my finger around it and kissed it, moving her hair aside so I could breathe more kisses up her shoulder to her neck.

"The tat is beautiful, it suits you. Any particular memory?"

She nodded. "Freedom. The end of a bad thing, the beginning of…the rest of my life." Her voice was flat, not inviting further questions. I understood the tragedy there. The Sanjay thing broke her heart, and she had a nice speech prepared to gloss over it. I've been there myself.

Moving on. I walked over to the shower stall, turning the hot water on full blast so it would get nice and steamy in here. The dogs were milling around wanting attention, so I invited them to leave and closed the door. Time to focus.

Facing her, I slid a hand across her cheek to the nape of her neck and tilted her face up for another kiss. Her pulse jumped under my thumb, and our eyes were so close, but then she nudged my lips apart with her tongue, inviting me to taste her again. And I did, exploring every inch of her mouth and nibbling on her lower lip, ravaging those full pink lips of hers and dying to do the same thing to her nipples. Instead I reached down to lift her pretty foot and kissed along the arch and her little toes. "How's your ankle?"

She flexed it a little and winced. "Still sore...but *that* feels good," she purred while I massaged the foot, finding a pressure point on her arch. The scent and feel of her was a tease that left me aching to be naked in the shower with her.

Finally I got my hands on those gorgeous breasts, tenderly I hoped, but shit, I couldn't wait to put my mouth on them. When she squirmed and arched into me, I lifted them and kissed one and then the other, her impossibly hard nipples getting even tighter. Kissing, sucking, licking with long strokes, I traced my fingers around the nipples, memorizing the sexy little bumps and the softness all around. Then I took a nipple in my mouth and sucked hard, pinching and twisting the other one.

Kissing her again, I loved the vibration of her moan, long and deep into my mouth. Can't lie, her response brings out the kinky caveman in me and I fought the image of my cock sliding effortlessly between her perfect tits pressed tight together, the head showing with each thrust. Totally inappropriate for that moment, but that's where my mind went. Just sayin'.

Ariana

His eyes bright with mischief, Javier pulled his soccer shorts below his navel, revealing the elastic of some tight-ish designer briefs he was wearing. Of course. His erection under there was so rigid it was bobbing against his belly, reaching up almost to the waistband. With a devilish smile, his voice rumbled low. "I'm going first again. One layer or two?"

"Oh, two, please." My voice sounded ragged, but I was glad to have found it at all after my breathy moaning. Dear God, I should be embarrassed, but he was so hot I didn't care. "Can I help?" I kissed that spot at the base of his neck, and then along the collarbone, enjoying the goosebumps that broke out across his muscled chest.

My thumbnail tweaked his nipple piercing again while my fingers traced the muscles and sprinkle of hair on his flat belly. I took my own sweet time about it, too, sliding off the counter and pulling both garments down to reveal that gorgeous cock of his. Hoooo, damn! Wanting to get a closer look, I sank to my knees, dipping my tongue in his navel on the way down and putting my hands on the hot, sleek skin of that raging hard-on. I took a deep breath, inhaling the scent of man, sweat and arousal. He was twitching, hands gripped at his sides when I ran a finger up the length of his erection, then followed with a sweep of my tongue. The room was so steamy at this point we were both damp.

His hands under my arms pulled me up and in, and he drew me closer and lowered his head, covering my lips in a demanding kiss. "I can't...you can't do that. Yet." His eyes were glassy, and I could feel his heart pounding against me. "I'm going to pull your pants down now and look at your pussy...because...because I've been thinking about it since

Saturday. And then…and then we'll get right in the shower, okay?"

When had the smooth-talking player turned into this guy? But I liked him. "Okay."

I put my hands on the waist of my shorts, but he stopped me. "Please let me do it." He knelt at my feet, dragging an open-mouthed kiss down my body until he was eye-level with my pussy. When he pulled down my shorts and panties, he just settled there, comfortable. "Damn. So beautiful." Staring again like he was when I took off my top, he apparently forgot we were supposed to get in the shower.

I could feel my face go hot, embarrassed that I hadn't showered yet, when he buried his face in my red, curly triangle. It didn't seem to bother him while he breathed me in, separating my outer lips with his fingers. He seemed driven to taste me, like he'd die if he didn't. And I didn't anticipate the mystical experience of his tongue on my clit, forcing me to hold tight to his shoulders because my legs were suddenly wobbly. "Mmmm, just a taste," he hummed, holding me steady while my head fell back, pleasure zinging through me. I could feel an orgasm building already, my cunt pulsing from his clever strokes.

I started to wonder if his other girlfriends had been bolder and more experienced, but never got to complete that thought. He scooped me up with a rough moan, as if he were interrupting himself. I found myself facing him in the shower, the water relaxing and energizing at the same time. "I'm starting to like being carried around all the time."

"Can you stand okay?" His dark hair had fallen forward, making him look messy and sexy.

I nodded, struck dumb again by his confident smile. "I'm good," I murmured and stood on tiptoe to kiss him, threading my fingers through his hair to uncover that handsome, chiseled face of his. He groaned into my mouth and his erection stirred against my belly, his lean body glistening under the stream of water.

I could've sworn I would come just from this kiss because, let's face it, I know a thing or two about kissing. Javier was, without a doubt, the best kisser I've ever encountered. There was no awkward dueling of tongues, or wondering which way to tilt your face, it's like those lips and teeth and tongue could read my mind or perhaps...*control* my mind. There was a focus there, the sting of his hands grasping my ass, focused on keeping me exactly where he wanted me so he could devour me. He held me so tightly my feet almost came off the floor when he ground into me. *Hot.* So hot it almost hurt. In the best possible way.

"Turn around," he said, pumping soap into his hands and working up a lather. "Let me enjoy you." I ached to touch him, to rub myself all over that beautiful brown skin and the solid muscles beneath. Truth be told, I'd pretty much directed the action in my other relationships. But I just turned around and braced my hands on the tile while he expertly sudsed my back and neck.

"That feels so good," I sighed. I was completely relaxed when he reached around to my breasts, playing with my nipples, his cock slick, resting between my ass cheeks. "Spread your legs for me, Ariana," he said, his voice husky.

Oooohhh, God. My head dropped back against his shoulder and I whispered, "Condom?"

Now his soapy fingers dropped to my pussy, his strong arms forcing mine to stay tightly at my sides while he teased my clit. "I'm not coming inside," he murmured, nipping my neck and adjusting his penis so it was sliding back and forth, stroking the outside of my pussy, gliding over my little nub every time he thrust forward.

It's hard to admit, but I thoroughly enjoyed being caged in by his arms, enjoying the way the Celtic tattoos on his biceps flexed with each stroke. "Mmmmmm…Uhhhhooohhh," my mindless pleasure sounds and his groans echoed off the walls, muffled by the streaming water. I felt the friction of his engorged head, and every vein in that thick cock sliding, slipping deliciously across my slit while waves of pleasure washed over me. I moved along with him, grinding into him and rotating my hips while he massaged my breasts.

Tweaking my nipples again, he spun me around when I started to tremble and scream. "Open your eyes *belleza*, I want you to look in my eyes when you come." He hooked a pair of thick fingers inside my channel, pressing the heel of his hand on my clit.

When I opened my eyes, I looked down first, wrapping my hand around his dick and stroking, letting my eyes wander up his gorgeous body to his face. The orgasm he was building with those talented fingers of his stunned me, hitching up and rising inside while the water tapped a steady rhythm on my skin. His eyes held mine, and I felt completely exposed, his other hand pinching and rolling my nipple until I exploded, contracting around his fingers with a low, shuddering cry. He wrapped his arms around me, holding me tightly until my trembling slowed, gently pressing my face against his chest and kissing the top of my head.

"Damn. Feeling you clutching my fingers like that. Crazy." Calmly and deliberately he turned me around again, massaging shampoo into my hair with those strong fingers of his. He took the handheld off and rinsed the shampoo out, running his fingers gently through my hair to take the tangles out.

I turned to him and put a hand on each side of his face. "That was…intense. But I don't understand. That felt so…intimate, like we've known each other for a long time. Is that how you are all the time?" He knew what I was really asking. *"Is that how you are with everyone?"*

I turned him around, going on tiptoe to shampoo *his* hair, and rinsing it, so he wouldn't have to look at me when he answered. He waited to answer until I was done, turning around and crushing my mouth to his for a long, breathless kiss. "No, I'm not usually like that." He was still hard as steel, his velvet cock poking my belly. "I feel it too."

I knew even then that it might have been a line. The ultimate line. The one that says, "You are special to me." But when I slid to my knees and took that hot cock in my mouth, I didn't care. I felt like the luckiest woman in Vegas.

Chapter Eight

Anne

IT WAS MOM'S birthday, and she was helping out at Tina and Taylor's house, her usual Thursday thing since Mama Tina's latest breast cancer recurrence.

I texted Ariana and asked, *Will u tell all?*

Ariana: *can't text. phone will melt.*

Anne: *not surprised. See u at T's?*

Ariana: *on my way. saw u on Owen's lap.*

Anne: *sexy laughs, kissed. He suddenly had to leave. WTF?!*

Ariana: *he say Y?*

Anne: *No. Left a glass slipper in the parking lot tho. Not.*

We have keys to Mama Tina and Taylor's house, and they have keys to ours, so I let myself into the kitchen. Taylor was reading at the kitchen table, and the house was quiet. When she put a finger to her lips, I sat next to her and pulled a book out.

"Mom is sleeping. Her bed is in the living room now," she whispered. That sounded bad to me; if Mama Tina couldn't even make it up the stairs anymore...

Familiar creaking from the basement stairs told us my

mom was coming up with clean laundry. "Hey, Susan," Tina said softly, "You didn't have to do that."

"It's my pleasure," Mom said. A chair scraped across the floor and we heard the crisp snap of a towel being folded. Taylor and I *were* reading, but we were conscious of the fact that we were also eavesdropping.

"I was thinking about Sara the other day. How's she doing, how's Steve?"

"Oh, Steve is home from Afghanistan for two weeks, but he and the baby are both sick, so Sara thought it best they not come around. Maybe next week?"

"I'd love that." The moms sat in companionable silence for a while. "I was thinking back to when I first met you, when you moved into my apartment building." Tina's voice was drowsy and faint. "Taylor was, what, three? The twins just turning one?" She sighed. "You were just frantic about Sara, about her being molested. Robert didn't know what was going on..." Taylor gasped and covered her mouth, reminding me to keep quiet. I shrugged and shook my head at her, letting her know this was news to me as well.

"Oh, you mean because he was drunk all the time? And that makes it okay that my husband's friend molested our daughter?!" There was a pause and then Susan said, "I'm sorry. I know that's not what you meant, Tina. Let me get you another pillow."

"It's okay, I know. I just think you need to be at peace about the incident with Sara. You didn't know, and you were doing what you had to do at the time. You were working full time after so many years, you had to."

"And remember how crazy it was with the twins? Ariana was always climbing on things. Remember when she fell out of the crib?"

Tina coughed, her voice hoarse. "And Anne had those ear

infections, one after the other, remember? Either you or I were always taking them to the pediatrician. It was total chaos back then." In the kitchen, Taylor and I had tears in our eyes, touched by the shock of the revelation about Sara and the intensity of these memories.

"Yes, I remember," Susan said. "I couldn't have gotten through it without you, Tina."

"Their first birthday party, remember that? We invited some kids in the building to that little apartment you were living in, and you made it so nice for them." There was no context for the images reeling through our heads; Ariana and I knew Dad was a drinker, but didn't really know him. We never knew about Sara, never knew we moved out of the house for a while.

"Until Robert crashed the party, smelling like liquor *again*." Her tone brighter at a different memory, Mom said, "We pretended it was Taylor's birthday too, remember?"

"Oh, my God, girl, we've been a great team, haven't we?" Tina started crying, and we heard the hospital bed creaking and scraping from the laughing and crying over their shared history.

Ariana didn't see us sitting at the table when she walked in the kitchen door. "Hey, Ma!" she yelled. "I brought your favorite birthday cake!" Certain that the moms wouldn't like that we overheard, we each put a finger to our lips and herded Ariana ahead of us, acting like we'd all arrived together. Tina and Mom were lying on the hospital bed together, currently whispering and giggling, not bothering to hide their tears.

"Happy Birthday, Mama Susan." Taylor walked the cake over to a table, stuck six candles in, and lit them.

"Let's celebrate!" I went back in the kitchen to get paper plates and forks.

"One candle for each decade," Mom joked.

We sang *Happy Birthday* and added a jazzy chorus of "And many mooooore!" at the end. Mom looked so pretty with the candlelight on her face, then she blew them out. We looked over at Tina and saw she'd fallen asleep. She had a big smile on her face.

Chapter Nine

Anne

I KEPT THINKING about Owen's kiss. No one talks about kissing, and I think it's totally underrated. But I had to admit kissing Owen was the most fun I'd ever had, and that got me to wondering about the clothes-off kind of fun.

When I confessed this to Ariana before bed, she said "Seriously, Anne, have you looked at any of the products we sell?"

"I have," I said, "but in more of a theoretical way or a numbers-on-a-spreadsheet way."

Lying in bed, I thought about how sex reminds me of wine. You have a glass of wine, and then you want another glass of wine, and then of course you want another glass, why the heck not? "Wheee, this is so fun!" you think, and then the next morning you wake up and you're soooo sick and you're soooo sorry.

It seems like sex is the same way. Ariana and my other friends get high on it, they can't get enough, they don't know when to stop and then…the crash, ohmygod, what a crash! The stay-in-bed-and-don't-shower-for-a-week kind of crash. It looks like it hurts, like you feel like an idiot. You hate yourself, telling yourself you were so stupid to fall for that, what were you thinking?

On the other hand, Owen has me thinking about what he looks like naked. Some men don't have to take off their shirts to give you a peek at their lean, sexy body. All they have to do is roll up their sleeves. First, there's that perfect amount of hair, that golden hair on his arms that I know I'd feel if I was naked and his arms were tight around me.

And then, don't get me started on the veins! Especially when Owen was going through that touch screen, sweeping through page after page, that blue ribbon of vein, and the taut, toned muscles in his forearm flexing and straightening. It wasn't enough that his low, gravelly voice stroked me like an invisible hand under my clothes…no, that alone made me lose my mind. But then he had to go and roll up his sleeves and show me the evidence, the reason why I get this feeling of power when I look at him.

At his job interview, I thought he just had great posture and a sexy voice. After focusing on the big, callused hands and the manly forearms, I couldn't stop thinking about the lean, ripped body that must be hidden under those clothes. I was hypnotized. Yup, officially losing it.

We'd been very flirty in the office since I sat on his lap Tuesday night, but suddenly I felt his fingers gripping my arms, pulling me up on my toes while he breathed a hot line of kisses along my jaw and down my neck. "I'm sorry Anne, I can't just be your friend. I wanted to, but I can't." He went deeper with his kiss, filling me with the sensation of his tongue, his teeth, his lips. He tasted just like I thought he would, different than anything, ever, and so yummy.

"Owen, I know. I want…" His lips covered mine, and he lifted me higher, and I wrapped my arms around his neck. He gasped, shocked, when I wrapped my legs around his waist, and he grabbed them and held them there.

This wasn't me, the horny woman who did things like this, but I couldn't think of a single reason not to. My flash of bravery was rewarded; I felt his erection growing, pressing against my panties, right...you know, right there. If I'd been braver, I'd have ground against him, shown him how good it felt, whispered in his ear that I could get myself off thinking about him. But of course I didn't.

He looked in my eyes, smiling, his gaze intense. "I guess you can tell I like you."

He didn't know how many times I'd sat at this very desk, touching myself and thinking about him.

I felt my heart pounding when he put his hand on my cheek and I leaned into it. Something sharp and unfamiliar ached between my legs, and I put my hands on his hips and pulled him in tight, grinding against him a little. "I'm kind of new at this. Show me what to do."

He stood straighter, clearing his throat and holding me at arm's length. "How new?"

When I thought about it later, this conversation was like Elsa icing up the town in *Frozen*. Owen's whole demeanor went stiff as a board. Oblivious, I continued to snuggle into him, avoiding his eyes. "Really new."

"So you've never...done...anything?"

"I've kissed and made out, you know, like you talked about the other night but...I've never...had sex."

When I looked up at him, he was pale and his eyes were so wide, like...shocked, and then he was rubbing his forehead with the back of his hand. "Anne, I don't know...maybe this is a bad idea. I had no clue."

Tears stung my eyes as he put me down, pulled up a chair and took my hand, folding it in his when he took a deep breath. "I've never…I mean I've heard it's huge for women when it's the first time, they have all these expectations. And look at you, you've waited, and you seem so serious, you're nervous and trembling like this is, uh, heavy duty for you. I can't, you know, be in a *serious*, committed relationship, I thought we just liked each other."

You know those moments in a movie when the world stops? This was my first real life world-coming-to-a-screeching-halt experience. *Ohmygod, how could I be so stupid, throwing myself at this guy? And I have to see him all the time. No way will he see me cry!*

Anger bubbled up in my gut, rapidly replacing shame. I stood and flung his hand back at him, brushing by him and turning when I was going out the door. "So it would've been okay for you to go home with that skank who hit on you at the bar, but it's too tough to be with me because I'm a virgin?!"

He just stood there with a dazed look on his face, his feet stuck to the floor.

After that day, we avoided each other in the office, suddenly very polite. I was glad Ariana was there. My cheeks were constantly hot with embarrassment—I'd offered myself and been turned down! At least once a day, he'd stop near me and take a breath as if he wanted to say something.

He texted me after work one day and asked if he could call, but unfortunately during the call he just kept digging that hole deeper. It was like he was trying to explain or rationalize it to himself.

"Just tell me something," he said. "This virginity thing is a big, big deal, right?"

"Pretty big, to me anyway."

"I read online that women have this perfect vision of how it's going to be and, you know, it's not usually like that. You'll be disappointed, won't you? You'll end up hating me."

"Where did you read that?" I realized he was still covering himself with silly camouflage, quoting whatever damn website backed up his theory, and hoping I would talk him out of his fear.

"If I was your first, I would always be your first, right? And that's a big responsibility, isn't it?"

I started crying, choking my words out into the phone. "I guess I hoped it wasn't some big responsibility, exactly." I had to stop and take a breath. "I was hoping you, meaning *you*, Owen... the guy I thought I liked and trusted...I was hoping you would think it was a privilege!"

And I hung up on him.

Chapter Ten

Anne

MY MOM IS psychic, how about yours?

I mean we live in the same house, but I'm out a lot, and so is she. How did she know to make my favorite dinner because I was feeling low? I followed my nose from our basement lair up to the kitchen, where she'd made roast beef, macaroni and cheese, and green beans. The cooking channel calls it comfort food, and I needed comforting so badly.

"Have you talked to Dr. Jobe lately?" she asked, putting a plate of food in front of me.

"No, but I guess I should, huh?" How did she know I needed to talk about the Wyatt incident from freshman year? "Mom, it's had an effect on me. Did you know I haven't...uh...?" My eyes filled with tears. She put her arms around me and rocked me a little.

"No sweetheart, I know you talk to your sister, and you saw the shrink, but no, I didn't know. I'm not surprised, though, after what happened." She held my face in her hands, smiling. "But you know it's okay, there's no crime in that, right?"

Fortified by the mac and cheese, I decided to finally call my therapist and make an appointment to talk about Wyatt. I emailed her ahead of time and told her I was going to vomit it out, and for her to pretend like it was a conversation, but not to actually interrupt me and ask questions, because it was going to be hard for me. Taylor knew about the attack, and she offered to drive and wait for me, drive me home in case I was upset.

At first I just talked with Dr. Jobe like I said I would and she nodded for me to keep talking. Then I looked up at the ceiling and told the whole story like I was watching a movie, pretending I was writing in my journal and no one would ever know.

"The whole thing started on Halloween. I hate Halloween! I'm a scaredy-cat at heart, and I feel sick when I see people walking around with bloody knives stuck in their head, or fake blood oozing out of their mouths. It gets worse when you go to college and stumble from bar to bar in fishnet stockings and kitty-cat ears, wondering why no one you meet seems to want to talk about the books you like to read or the music you listen to.

"But honestly? What guy is going to do that when your tits are hanging out of your pirate bustier? Aaargh! So anyway, doc, this rant was meant to explain why I showed up to meet my friends on Halloween dressed as a flasher. That's right, a flasher. I wasn't in the mood to think about dressing up for Halloween, so I procrastinated about a costume until the very last minute. At first, I thought the trench coat, the sunglasses and the boots in my closet could be a spy costume, but for some reason everyone thought I was a flasher. This is the main problem with ambiguous Halloween costumes—people can project their own kinky delusions onto your hastily thrown-together outfit.

"Speaking of hasty, I forgot to write down the name of the bar where I was meeting my friends, but I thought I knew which one it was. When I got there at nine, I didn't see anyone I knew, but figured they were running late. Since I hadn't eaten, I sat at the bar and ordered a beer to justify scarfing down handfuls of peanuts.

"That's when the drunk guy next to me identified me as a flasher. 'C'mon, c'mon, flash me!' the guy slurred, reaching for the top button of my trench coat. 'Whas' under there?'

"Then someone behind me said, 'Excuse me, sir, I think the young lady would rather not take off her coat.' The guy who came to my rescue was Wyatt. 'Sir, let me take your drink over to that table over there, so you can leave her alone.' He actually got the guy situated elsewhere, and then came back and sat down next to me.

"'Thank you,' I said, grateful and thinking he was pretty smooth. I started babbling, telling him I might be at the wrong bar, and asking silly questions like 'Why do we think spies wear trench coats? They're just fancy raincoats. Do they hang out in the rain for some reason?'

"Anyway, it was a funny way to meet someone, eating peanuts at the wrong bar, dressed as a spy/flasher. It was such a cool beginning to such an awful relationship! Thing is…from the moment I met him, I felt insecure, and it wasn't the outfit. And the first time, THE VERY FIRST TIME I said something about my feelings, he dismissed them. I should have known right then that he was going to get off on making me feel like shit.

"But it was hard, you know? He was good-looking, he worked out, he had nice friends, was a prestigious business major, and had a cool apartment with a balcony. You know, ticked all the boxes. Looked good on paper. I held on to him for dear life, feeling a desperate longing to make it work. But I knew something wasn't right, there was no…spark. Yeeees, that was it. His kisses were clumsy, and he wanted me to make out with him without making out with me, if you know what I mean. Instead of going from zero to sixty, I couldn't get past ten. He said it was silly that I wasn't ready to have sex with him, I must be frigid. It was the worst six months of my life.

"But I kept trying. Maybe I thought he was the best I could do, the last guy out there. Or at least the last guy who would put up with me. When I finally said maybe we should break up, he got possessive on me and paid attention for a while. BIG clue there that I totally missed.

"At one point I talked to my big sister Liz about it, and wondered, 'Is it possible that some people just don't fit, you know, sexually? If the foreplay is rushed or just awkward, won't the sex be awkward?'

"'Oh, my God,' Liz said, 'I know just what you mean. From my experience, that should lead to an awkward—but necessary—breakup. This guy is disrespecting your feelings. Get away from him ASAP. In other words, RUN!'

"Anyway, I broke up with him. He was ugly about it, on the one hand telling me he didn't care, good riddance, and on the other hand blackmailing me emotionally. When he threatened to tell our mutual friends that I was a frigid, virginal freak, I shot back that I'd do the same, hinting that Wham-Bam-Wyatt had the rushing game down.

"I'm sorry, but that was just a mean thing he pushed me with, so I pushed back. Everyone who knows me knows I hate bullies. 'Here's how it is,' I remember saying, play-acting it for him, pretending to tell a secret, 'Wyatt wants to get to home plate without taking a run around the bases.'

"Something about the way he reacted told me that not only had I hit humiliation pay dirt, but that I wasn't the first one to say it about Wyatt.

"I went to bed early the Thursday after the breakup, 'cause I knew he'd be at the frat party that night; it was his fraternity, the same one Sanjay belonged to. Ariana was there with Sanjay. I hadn't told her I broke up with Wyatt yet, so I was tucked up in my dorm bed alone.

"Wyatt used the key card I'd given him, came in while I was sleeping at 2 am. He was drunk, but managed to get all the way into my dorm room before I heard him say 'You can't break up with me, you fuckin' witch, you're not good enough to break up with me.'

"If you ever see the evidence photos, you'd have to agree that he got the worst of it. I had a black eye and ugly bruises on my neck from when he was on top of me trying to choke me, sure, but I don't think he was expecting me to scratch right through the skin on his eyelids and down his face, taking the skin with it. I gave him a pretty good shot to the balls, but the scratches really pissed him off.

We both took a nasty fall when I got out from under him and made a run for the door. He grabbed my foot, but I was moving fast enough that we both went down hard, and he broke his nose, getting blood all over the floor. 'Goddamn you, goddamn you to hell!' I heard him scream, knowing he was upset about the damage to his pretty face.

I made it down the hall to my floor proctor's room and, thank God, the door was open, and I got in and closed the door quietly behind me before he saw where I went. 'Call campus police!' I whispered to her, and they arrived in time to catch Wyatt, who was running down the street holding a towel to his nose. Jack and Cole were in England, so I called Liz on my way to the security office to identify him.

"'Identify him as your attacker and don't say anything else until I get there!' Liz counseled. I could see why, because the campus people were already trying to soft-pedal the attack, not wanting to create unwanted publicity about violence and date-rape for the university.

"'Now, Anne, I know you're upset, but these things just happen after a breakup. You said he didn't rape you, right?' An administrator was trying to calm me down after I identified Wyatt and made sure he was locked up.

"I was livid. 'No, but that was his intent! And *what* fucking things *just happen* after a break-up?' I pointed to my rapidly-darkening eye and the bruises on my neck. 'People get punched in the eye and strangled, is that what *just happens*?!'

"At that point, Liz, Ariana, and a man I didn't know burst through the door. 'Anne, sit down, relax. We've got this,' Liz said. 'Hey, Mr., uh, Putnam,' she said, checking the administrator's name tag, 'We'd like to talk with Anne for a couple of minutes, and then we'll be right with you.'

"'Well, I don't know,' Putnam huffed, 'We should really...'

"Liz stopped him cold. 'Mr. Putnam, this is our attorney, by the way, Josh Levine.'

"It was comical how quickly Putnam shut up and left us alone after that. And because of Liz's quick thinking and persuasive manner, we actually got Wyatt charged with felony battery and put in jail for a year. If not for that, he would've gotten off with a misdemeanor and been back on campus in a month. There was no way the university couldn't expel him after the real trial that followed, and his actions are now on his permanent record. Most of Wyatt's 'friends' didn't like him anyway, so they were relieved about having an excellent excuse to stop hanging out with him. It also helped that, lo and behold, he had a previous assault complaint from a woman two years before, when he was a freshman. Asshole! We heard when he got out of jail, but a year had passed since then, and we didn't see him around.

"But I hadn't counted on the fear, shame, anger, and grief that hit me once the excitement died down. I felt out of it, moving in slow motion, and unable to complete even the simplest tasks. Binge-watching *Law and Order* was the only thing that made me feel better at first, partly because it's great and it's always on, and partly because the 'special victims' on the show had even worse things happen to them and they survived. Some even seemed to thrive. Ariana kept a close eye on me. In fact, I think that's why she didn't pick up on the fact that her boyfriend was engaged to someone else.

"I dreamed about the attack for months, and that's when we moved out of the dorm and back in with Mom. Mom was a little upset that she wasn't the first person I called that night, but Liz's expert response made it seem like the right move. 'We know that it takes a village, Mom,' Liz said to her. 'Luckily, you gave birth to a big village.'

"The only thing left now is that I've still been avoiding any kind of relationship with a guy. But now I met someone and I…" Out of breath, I paused.

I hadn't stopped talking the whole time, and Dr. Jobe was smiling at my sudden hesitation.

"Maybe you weren't avoiding a relationship, Anne. Maybe some time had to pass, that's all. Maybe you just had to meet the *right* guy. You don't strike me as a woman who always needs a boyfriend, am I right?"

"That's absolutely true." They were so nice, her comments. Talking to me like a normal person, not a victim. Maybe I was a normal person. "No, I definitely don't need a boyfriend to be happy. Only had one, and look how that ended. But I'm ready…I may have already blown it, but I'm definitely ready for this one."

Chapter Eleven

Anne

OWEN ALWAYS MOVES like a man who knows where he's going, smooth, confident and quick. That day was the exception though, and his face was flushed while he shifted from one foot to the other in front of my desk. "These are for you," he said, holding a huge bunch of my favorite white jasmine flowers, the ultrafeminine blossoms looking even more girly in his big, work-roughened hands.

It was the end of the work day, and we'd both been busy, so I was still in extreme politeness mode.

"Owen, thank you, what's up? Those are my favorite! You...how did you know?" I asked.

He didn't answer me right away, but it was obvious he had some kind of a plan, purposefully putting the flowers in a pitcher I kept in the adjoining bathroom and placing them on my desk.

That lopsided grin I love, the one I'd been missing so much, spread across his face. "Uhhh...I looked at your bio on the website, the one where you list your favorite things?"

We both laughed, and I forced myself to look up at him. The warm, flowery scent surrounded us when he took my hand, pulling me up and out of my chair and into his arms to kiss the side of my neck.

"I bought them because I wanted to show you that today is special."

"Why is that?" I felt myself quivering against him. "Why is today special?" THAT THING was hanging in the air again, the whole conversation about my stupid virginity.

"Because today is the beginning...the beginning of us. If you still want it to be." He smiled at me and kept planting little kisses on my face, leaning away and looking in my eyes when I giggled. "What? What's funny?"

I closed my eyes and hid my face in his chest, pulling him close. "So I guess you decided I'm worth it, worth the big responsibility?" I tried to force more sarcasm into those last two words, but my voice was too wobbly.

"Oh, my God, yes!" he chuckled, his voice gentle and low. "It wasn't really...I just never...I talked to Javier about it, and he told me I was an idiot." He kissed my hand and dragged me out to the picnic table, smiling when I struggled to keep up with his long strides.

The pink desert sunset called to us, and he gestured to the little grove in the back of the building, and I saw the two trees surrounding the picnic area twinkling with white Christmas lights wrapped around the trunks. He'd covered the table with a folded white sheet and a pair of white pillar candles flickered on paper plates. "So...what do you think?"

I kind of wanted to cry at how sweet he was being, picturing this big, serious dude out here lighting candles and decorating trees for me. Now he was being bashful, rubbing the back of his head and then cramming his hands into his pockets. It was the sweetest thing anyone had ever done for me, and I was speechless. All I could think of to do was nestle in my new favorite place, nuzzling my cheek into his chest.

"You are so fucking sweet, and I want you so much. I'm sorry I was an ass." He pressed two fingers below my chin, guiding my face back up to look at him. "I care about you, and I was afraid I'd screw it up. I want this to be perfect for you, but I'm far from perfect."

I felt tears coming to the surface, tears of regret and happiness at the same time. "I felt lonely avoiding you." I felt my lips trembling and I confessed, "I missed you, being friends with you."

Wincing, he held me tighter to him and whispered "I'm sorry" in my ear again.

He chuckled while he hurried to the other side of the table, where a big box full of Chinese takeout from Wok Me, my favorite place, magically appeared. Then Owen pulled icy bottles of Kirin beer, two real plates, and some cloth napkins out with a flourish, and we sat down across from each other, gobbling up the Xinjiang noodles he knows I love while we talked and talked, the lights and candles twinkling around us. He asked me about school and soccer, and we talked about *So You Think You Can Dance*, the dance show we always liked to watch together on his laptop, right here on this picnic table, while we had lunch. He covered my hand with his. "I missed doing this with you."

When he opened up the tiny steamed dumplings I always order, he sat next to me and pulled me onto his lap with a wolfish grin. "Let me feed these to you." I started to shake my head, laughing, but he pressed it to my lips with his chopsticks.

Holy cow! Who knew having someone feed you could make your panties wet? His eyes were fierce, his voice husky, when he fed me another bite and growled, "Mmmmm. The only thing I like more than your lips is that little pink tongue of yours."

He could definitely feel I was turned on, squirming on his lap, and he buried his face in my neck the way he'd done at Sparky's.

Then he straightened, clearing his throat. Looking very uncomfortable, he said, "So when I talked to Javier, one of the things he said was that of course you want your first time to be special, so I should just kick myself in the ass and make it special. So…uh…I reserved a special hotel room for us. Do you want to go there?

"When?" My panties were getting a little damp from all this talk of "specialness."

"How about tomorrow night after soccer?"

I squeezed his shoulders and gave him a silly peck on the cheek. "Okay." The minute I left the office I started to text Ariana, but she called me first.

Chapter Twelve

Anne

WHEN WE WERE tiny, redheaded terrors, we often said the same exact thing at the same time. It was usually a basic-human-needs phrase like "Want a cookie!" or "Hafta go bafroom!" and Mom called it twin sync. Now, as adults, we do it at moments of high emotion, both happy and sad, and occasionally while calling and texting. We learned in psychology that it's actually a *thing* and it's called 'synchronicity' but it was still weird when it happened.

Ariana called me and gushed, "I am so…happy, I can hardly stand myself. I swear, Javier lights up when I walk in the room, and he calls me to make plans. Is this the crazy little thing called love?"

I was stunned silent, but recovered enough to say, "Can I send you the text I was just about to send you? Give me a sec, it's in draft now."

I heard her gasp when she received it, and then she read it out loud.

"I swear, Owen lights up when I walk in the room, and he apologized and made plans for us to go to a hotel tomorrow night after soccer. Is this that crazy little thing called love?"

Not only had we made the same observations, but we'd used the same Queen song to describe it. Now, that's synchronicity!

Laughing at ourselves for a good five minutes, I added, "I can't stop smiling! The sun is shining, we're graduating, and I'm finally going to have actual sex with an actual man!"

"Wait!" Ariana. "Next you were going to say 'And he actually likes me and may want to have sex with me again!' Right?"

It was true, and we hadn't laughed together like this for a looong time *Why was that?* I filed the question away in my mind to answer some other time.

"So I'll see you later?" Ariana said.

"Of course! I'm excited, but…you know, nervous about, you know, with Owen. Will it hurt a lot?"

"Why are you asking that? Do you think we have identical vaginas?" We both laughed again. "Anyway, my first time I got, uh, a little sore, but it was still exciting. You remember Marty, right, junior year of high school?"

"Of course. You were on that green couch in the basement and I was keeping watch in case Mom came home from work early." I hesitated but pressed on. "Did he get you off? Was he any good?"

"Oh, my gawd, of *course* not! He barely got the condom on before he came. High school dickwads don't have the slightest idea how to get a girl off! But by the time we were seniors, we'd trained each other up nicely. Workin' on the night moves, right? I was thinking about taking on a trainee before I met Javier. Now *I'm* the trainee. And by the way, something tells me Owen's going to be nothing like Marty. The man has…like, slow hands, and a slow burn under that sexy, nerdy exterior of his."

"Hey, watch what yer sayin' about my boyfriend!" We

laughed at my gum-chewing tough girl imitation. "Unrelated question, though. My phone is heating up lately, and I run out of charge quickly all of a sudden. Are you seeing any of that?"

"No. Same old. Take it to the phone store at the mall?"

"Yeah, maybe I'll do that."

Chapter Thirteen

Javier

THE JOKE BETWEEN guys is, the girl who can't wait to take your pants off is a hookup, the girl who washes your pants is a girlfriend.

But that's just lame. In my mind, it's so obvious. If we have nothing to talk about, it's a hookup. If I can't stand to be away from her for more than a day, she's my girlfriend. And I feel that way about Ariana. I've had a couple of girlfriends, in high school and beyond, and even had a fiancée once.

I mean, think about how awesome she is. Ariana and Anne started a soccer team to keep in touch with friends. Now it's a huge deal, it's a fucking league, with a website, and hundreds of people participating.

Then they created this retail site, *Two Much*, as a project for a marketing class, and they've actually made it work. In fact, it's a very successful business. It even has a conscience, with eco-friendly toys, and lotions, and a lot of honest information about contraception and such. Who knew that half of all pregnancies in the US aren't planned? No glove, no love, people! Crazy.

And speaking of crazy, tonight we played against a pot-smoking team that calls themselves the Wing Nuts.

The Wing Nuts play loud stoner music like "Burn One Down," and their moves are kind of a cross between Bob Marley and Homer Simpson, things that only seem smart when you're really stoned, which they were. Like in most of the first half, they decided they would only kick the ball as hard as they could, and just see where it went, and then they got into kind of a kick-about, not directing it at the goal.

The last quarter they decided they'd only drive the ball down the center of the field. It actually turned out fairly well for them, 'cause it took us a while to figure out what they were doing, but we did beat them in the end.

The women Wing Nuts were especially fun, with lots of tattoos and piercings. Ariana gave me the stink eye when one of them started rubbin' up on me, but, hey! *Que no pare la fiesta*, don't stop the paaaaarty!

Ariana

I saw him. I saw goddamned Wyatt, and I didn't know what to do. If Anne found out he was watching her, she'd freak out. He was sitting on the bleachers watching our soccer game, wearing a Yankee ball cap like a million other guys. But he's *not* a million other guys, he's the bastard who attacked my sister, was convicted, and went to jail for it.

Wasn't it against some kind of law for him to be there? I guess we still have mutual friends, so that's probably how he found out about the game.

If I talk to Javier or Owen, they'll get up in arms and want to beat the guy up and get Anne upset. Mom's got her hands full with Tina, Jack and Cole are away at sea. Liz. I'll call Liz.

I took a time-out and sent in a substitute for the second half of the game, and, thank God, Liz answered right away. Leaning against the back of the Rita's Margarita's truck, I filled her in.

"I'll call Josh. Remember him, the lawyer?" she said. "Anyway, he'll probably recommend a restraining order, like Wyatt has to stay X amount of distance away, but we have to show he's a danger first." I described his current behavior, and she said, "It's kind of weird, isn't it? He's been out of jail for a while, and suddenly he's out in the open?"

I sucked in a breath, suddenly realizing the why of the situation. "Damn, maybe he's been watching her for a while, but now she's seeing Owen, he's pissed. I've always thought that's what brought on the attack when she broke up with him, that he couldn't stand the thought of her with another guy." I felt physically sick just thinking about it, nauseous enough to throw up.

"We can probably get the restraining order, but here's the problem: sometimes it just pisses the guy off, and if he's delusional, he'll ignore it anyway."

"I'm curious, Liz. How do you know so much about this stuff?"

"I had to, uh, look into it for a client...and besides, don't you watch cop shows on TV? Don't you get creeps freaking up your website?"

"Probably, but luckily Owen handles that." I often had the feeling Liz was exercising selective disclosure when she talked about her business, but I guess that's how things work. "So you got this for now? I'll talk to her about it tomorrow."

"Why tomorrow?"

I mean, Liz is our sister, I reasoned, so she can know. "Anne and Owen are going to spend the night together, in a suite at the Mandarin."

"NO WAY!" Liz knew what that meant.

"Way." I said.

Together we both said "Finally."

Javier

Ariana sat on the sidelines for the last part of the game, then gave her sister a big hug, gesturing excitedly and whispering in her ear while they walked away.

Owen and I followed behind. I don't know Owen that well, just well enough to get the impression that he follows the guy conversation rules: 1) Get to the point. 2) Don't get too personal. 3) Don't one-up me unless you're looking for a fight.

I handed him a beer from Rita's truck. "So…things are good with you two? You doin' that thing we talked about?"

I laughed when he nodded and gave me a slap on the back.

"Thanks, man," he said. As I suspected, Owen knows and skillfully follows the guy rules. "Sooo…," he continued after a swig of beer, "what does that mean exactly, that you're asking me if we're good?"

"It means you and I are in a relationship too, kind of, doesn't it?"

"I hope that's true man, I really hope that's true," and we laughed and clinked beer cans. For a quiet guy, he did get right to the point. I got the meaning behind the question, that he's already protective of Anne, 'cause I feel the same way about Ariana.

Guys don't need bullet points; we just need to know if the playing field is open.

Chapter Fourteen

Anne

I WASN'T SURE if my mind was as ready to go as my body, but Owen and I headed out together holding hands. "Do I need, you know, different clothes or whatever?" Knowing him, he didn't want to make fun of me, but I could see he was trying not to laugh. Blushing, I giggled, "I guess the idea is no clothes, huh?" and he opened the door to his truck and helped me in.

He leaned in, his face even with mine, his green eyes glowing. "You with no clothes on is the best idea, ever."

On the way over, he took my hand over the console. "So…tell me about what's-his-name, your ex-boyfriend. Only if you want to. You've said he was a dick but…what did you guys, uh, do exactly?"

I looked straight ahead and spoke shorthand in a tone that sounded empty even to me. "Wyatt was my only, like, physical boyfriend. He wanted to have sex, said I was frigid when I said I wasn't ready. We got naked a couple of times, tried oral. I hated it. I was too self-conscious, and he held my head and I gagged. Too much detail?" I didn't tell him the violent and unspeakable ending of course. Why would I?

Shaking his head and scowling, Owen squeezed my hand. "No, uh, perfect amount. Did you guys laugh at all, any good times, or...what? I guess since he was a psycho jerk, it doesn't sound like it."

"I wouldn't have imagined that laughing could even be a part of it until this moment." I picked up his hand and kissed it. "But I can totally imagine that with you."

It turns out that when Owen says something is special, it is REALLY SPECIAL. An hour after he took my hand and walked me to his truck, I found myself putting on a luxurious white cloud-soft robe. I was in a suite at the Mandarin Oriental, arguably the most swankified hotel on the Las Vegas strip, and I walked out of the bedroom into the fanciest bathroom *any*one has ever seen *any*where. Floor to ceiling windows in front of a large sunken tub framed a view of the Las Vegas strip. I stopped to look out at the thousands—no millions—of twinkling lights and high definition screens out there, a sight that made me finally understand why people think this town I've lived in my whole life is so magical. Then I heard someone get into the tub behind me. Hopefully Owen.

The sexy guy in the tub *was* Owen, but a more intense version of Owen. "I've got a glass of your favorite wine here with your name on it." When I started to walk toward him he said, "You have to take your robe off first, and let me see you standing in front of that window."

Okay, time to man up, I told myself. *Maybe I should say Wonder Woman up, or Buffy up or Ariana up.* I felt myself flushing hot under my freckles, but took my robe off anyway, letting it slide slowly down my naked body like I imagined a bold woman would.

His jaw was set tight, his lips pressed together like he was holding himself back. Licking his lips, he asked, "Do you have any idea how beautiful you are, Anne?" in a husky voice.

Now let's face it, every woman wants to hear that, doesn't she? I glanced at myself in the mirrors to the right of the tub and struggled not to judge, but I could tell he meant it. His eyes were dark and shining in a way I'd never seen before. I slid into the water next to him, looking out at the incredible view and drinking wine that tasted delicious, like…oh, I don't know…cupcake flowers, maybe?

My breasts floated up to the surface while we sipped wine and touched each other. When I told him about the cupcake flowers, he laughed. "You're right, that's exactly what it tastes like." I was dying to ask how much this suite cost and how he could afford it, but I knew it would mess with the wicked perfection of this moment.

His kisses were wild and uninhibited while he explored my mouth, tweaked my nipples, and let me touch him under the water, seeming to understand it was the first time I ever allowed myself to relax and explore that crazy thing that men are so (dare I say it?) attached to. He felt me tense up at first and whispered, "You will expand too, it will be okay. Try to relax."

It was very large and very hard…and kind of exciting, honestly. "I guess you guys are old friends," I said, watching the stormy look that crossed his face when I touched him.

"Oh, yeah," he said, his voice raspy.

"If I had an awesome toy like that, I guess I'd play with it too," I giggled again, suddenly understanding why guys are always adjusting themselves. The mystery was right there for me, under the water, the veins and ridges swelling and contracting when I touched and stroked while his lips and teeth closed around my nipples.

His fingers kept a steady pressure on my clit, and I arched

toward them as he moved in circles, pinching, pressing and pushing a finger slightly in *there*. "Whew," he breathed in my ear, "You are slick, so ready for me."

Without breaking our kiss, he pulled me on top of him, and I got breathless and even more excited when his hardness was against me—not inside, but so close. I'd never gone this far before. There I was, naked and exposed, inches from his face, but I was starting to understand what all the fuss was about. Rocking against his fingers, I slid back and forth, making my own little tsunami in the tub while he flicked my nipple with his tongue and then drew it in, sucking on it.

"It's okay, Annie, let go. Show me how you come." I heard myself making little sex noises and threw my head back and came, "Huheeehhhohhhh," amazed I was able to do that in front of him.

He held me while I calmed down, easing down into the bubbling water so I wouldn't get cold, and I felt tears in my eyes. He had just shown me what I was capable of. I was actually able to go bold and hot with a man who took the time to find what turned me on.

Yay! Maybe I'm not a frigid virgin bitch after all!

Why did I feel so free, so much less inhibited than I was with he-who-shall-remain-nameless? Was it the wine, the fancy suite, the water? No, it was because it was Owen. He was totally thrilled to be there with me, awkward inexperience and all, and I absolutely knew it was true, because his heart was pounding fast under my hands.

He climbed out of the water on the window side, his broad shoulders outlined against the night while he stood there, holding a towel for me. "Come here, Annie. Let me take care of you." I caught another shadowy glimpse of myself reflected in the mirror, my lips swollen from his kisses, my nipples standing at attention. My breathing was still ragged, and I was shaking, but enjoying the drag of the towel when he rubbed me all over with it, drying and massaging me at the same time.

Owen

She looked so satisfied and relaxed when she got out of that tub, so sweet. I just held her tight, wrapped up in the towel. We stood naked looking out over the city, relaxed from the water, the wine and, in her case, a huge orgasm.

She took my hand and led me over to the bed, blushing when she looked up at me. I couldn't help but laugh when she said "I'm nervous, but I'm ready."

"I'm ready too, but first I want to taste you." She looked worried when I said that, so I laid her head on some pillows and kissed her, admiring her gorgeous red hair fanned out on the bed. I touched her all over and got her worked up again, till her eyelids were heavy and her hands clutched the blanket.

That sweet triangle of red hair was pointing right at the current center of my universe, and when I licked her thigh and inhaled the sweet smell of her, she arched off the bed with a moan.

"I...uh, couldn't come that way when, uh...before." I could tell she felt bad about it, like she'd failed somehow.

"You don't have to come, you just have to let me eat you and enjoy you." I put her hand on my stiff cock. "This is how excited I feel about licking that sweet pussy of yours. I could eat you all night."

"OhhOOOhh," she cried out after about two minutes, her eyes bright while she watched me lick her wet slit. Using fingers, lips and tongue, I was sucking, licking and thrusting my tongue inside her until she started grinding against my mouth. She was also watching us in the mirror angled above the bed.

Her head started to thrash back and forth, her voice raw when a scream exploded from somewhere deep inside. It was even more of a rush, because I had already discovered she was responsive, and knew she was going to come big time. When I sucked on her clit hard, she went stiff and fell apart, her heels digging into the bed. I got off on watching her come, she looked so hot. "Oh God, oh God, Owen…ohmygod!"

I turned away a little, rolling on a condom and putting lubricant on it before I pressed her legs apart and leaned over her. "You still sure about this?" I asked, knowing I might die if she said no. She answered me with a savage kiss, tasting herself and saying "Yes, yes," while she pulled me down on top of her.

Pulling her knees up a little, I told her to take a deep breath and pressed into her pretty hard the first time. I read online that it was better that than dragging out the uncomfortable part. Her eyes opened wide and she froze, gazing up at me and breathing through the pain while she got used to the feel of me being inside. My heart was pounding and I was sweating, wanting to fuck her hard and fast, but forced myself to stay still, stroking her face. "You. Are. So. Tight." I choked out, "You okay?"

I made only tiny movements, sliding in and out a little until she relaxed enough to answer. "It's…it was more of a sharp pinch…and now it feels…I feel kind of full. Full of you." She smiled then, and it went right to my heart. I felt her stretch around me while I pushed in, clutching me so tightly I had to bite my lip not to come.

"Let's go real slow, Miss Annie, and I like it when you tell me how it feels, what you want." I grinned and kissed her freckles. "We had only moaning, screaming yes! and ohmigod! for a while there, but I like when you talk even better." Until I heard my own words, I wasn't conscious of how much I like her voice and her talkative nature.

She was looking up in the mirror again, and I started easing in, over and over, and circling my hips, then pulling back, until I started to feel her quiver inside, like she was going to come again. "Mmmm, you're liking that already aren't you?"

"Can't talk, don't make me talk," she whispered, "I just want more of you and...and more of this."

I picked up the rhythm again, and she was panting now, whimpering and saying "Please, Owen, pleeeease." The sight of her there, her legs wide open for me and her breasts bouncing, was spectacular. I can't believe I almost passed this up. It was like we had always known each other and there was this feeling, an intense feeling. It made me want to savor everything about this experience.

"You want to come again, sweet girl, and so do I," I watched her teeth clamp down on her lower lip. "Look into my eyes, and we'll come together." I pushed in short strokes, struggling not to hurt her, and we both fought to keep our eyes open, to be there with each other.

She tightened like a knot again, a strangled cry escaping from her lips. I pressed in again and stayed there, pure, hot pleasure rushing through me whenI let go and came, moaning "Anne, Anne, uhhh, mmmm."

I collapsed next to her while I tried to catch my breath. She seemed to rally, kissing my forehead, my cheeks, my mouth, and my eyes, then tracing her fingers through the hair on my chest.

Anne

I couldn't get enough of him, all that muscle and warm skin. I enjoyed nuzzling around his neck and twirling his hair around my fingers. I ran my fingers over his tattoo, a tribal he says means "unlimited." He let me explore his feet, massaging and staring at them, which was cool because, as you've probably noticed, men's feet are really different. When he was on top of me, I loved watching his muscles while he thrust in and out.

You know, you get to a certain age, I'm gonna say age seven, and you go on kind of a hugging and kissing strike. You want to decide who touches you, and my mom was cool with that. But the net result is that overall you don't get touched as much, though Ariana and I often slept in the same bed, and our family are big huggers whether you want to or not. I climbed on top of him, putting my pussy right in that spot again, and gave him a big smile. "Tonight I am a woman. And now I get to touch you anywhere whenever I want."

He tried to frown but couldn't, a slow smile breaking out across his face. "Welllll, maybe not *whenever* you want."

I pretended to be scared. "Huh! You're not going to check your phone and run out of here like your pants are on fire are you? Running away to wherever it is you run away to?" (Okay, I wasn't totally pretending.)

He usually clams up when I bring that up, but not this time. "I'm…uh…the superintendent of the building I live in. I'm supposed to be there by midnight, but I got someone to cover my…uh…shift."

No doubt looking to change the subject, he asked, "Are you sore? Does it hurt to do that?" I was feeling my power, sliding around and getting wet again while he was starting to, mmmm, grow.

"I probably need to wait an hour until we do that again," I said, putting my hand on him instead.

"You are so hot, and you feel as fantastic as you look," he breathed into my ear, giving my ass a squeeze. "Wait a minute, I'll be right back." I'm sure he peed and got rid of the condom, coming back with a lovely warm, wet cloth and a towel to clean off my sensitive flesh.

I saw him check me out between my legs and I asked "Was there blood?"

"None that I can see. Looks like you're fine," he murmured, his shoulders relaxing when he lay down next to me. "So...was it..." He was suddenly mute, looking kind of vulnerable.

"It was everything I hoped for, but better," I said, kissing his forehead. I felt...boneless, my legs like jelly.

"Better how?" he asked, his head propped up on an elbow.

Guys always want details. They seem to need to quantify, know what I'm sayin'?

"So you want a report card, a spread sheet, what?" I replied, and he laughed. I took his hand and rested it on my belly, which felt warm and good, 'cause I was a little crampy. "It was better because...I didn't realize...I didn't understand about the emotional connection I would feel while doing this. Is it okay to say that? Does it make you want to run and hide?"

Owen pulled me in and kissed me, not tentative and not tough, just...perfect. I pressed my hands on his chest, ready to follow one compliment with another. "You are a helluva kisser, do you know that?"

He gave me his crooked smile, like he knew an answer might incriminate him. He seemed so comfortable in his own skin, I envied him. "I would ask how you know the way to every sensitive spot on my body, but do I really want to know?"

Surprisingly, he answered. "I'll give you the short answer, like you gave me earlier. A woman in the neighborhood who I did yard work for. A few girlfriends in high school and college, but nothing serious. Some hookups, I gotta admit. A relationship two years ago, right before I met you. No one lately. That's my entire sexual history."

"OOOhhhh, the older woman," I purred, moving backward down his legs. He propped himself up on his elbows, watching me. "Did she do *this* to you?" I said, putting his erection between my breasts and squeezing them together, moving back and forth, letting that purplish head pop out, and feeling his breath coming fast and shallow.

"Yes," he gasped, "but, damn, where did *you* learn it?!" Now *he* was looking in the mirror above the bed and I was naked and unashamed. Yay, me! He sat up straight and ran his fingers down my back to cradle my butt cheeks in his big hands, gently guiding me.

"Porn, of course," I said, taking him in my hand now and fondling his balls. They were kind of scratchy, and one of them kept hiding, but I was so proud of myself I could barely stand it. I saw this online and wondered if I'd ever be able to actually do it, but here I was, doing it. I was just getting the concept of wanting to give the other person the pleasure they gave you, and I imagined us doing all kinds of filthy things for hours. "I love smelling you and hearing the noise you make when you come. I want to watch you come, I dreamed about it."

"What else?" he asked, fighting for breath.

"I tasted myself when you kissed me, and now I want to taste you. I want to taste everything." I sent a quick prayer to the goddess of blow jobs, and had my first taste of the salty liquid on the tip, then licked and kissed that impressive member of his. He groaned softly and I got giddy, thinking I must be a natural as I crawled off and knelt beside him. Sheer physics seemed to dictate that I could get more of him in my mouth this way than the other way, but I wished I could tie up my hair and get it out of my way.

I had a stroke of genius (here we go with the puns again), gathered my hair into a ponytail and put his hand around it near the scalp. I know he loves to touch my hair, and he confirmed it, shuddering. "Hold onto that for me, will you?" I drawled, batting my eyelashes at him while I lowered my mouth around his very erect shaft.

He could now see my face and know I had no idea what I was doing, but I quickly figured out that I should make my mouth work like my pussy, tightening my lips around his dick, sucking and heading south until the head almost hit my throat and staying there. His body bucked a bit, his delectable abs grew taut, and his moans of pleasure were getting louder.

His grip tightened on my hair, and I briefly put my hand up around his fist and pushed down, wordlessly asking him to direct the rhythm. First of all, I saw it in porn and second, I didn't have a clue how fast to go. I knew I should hate it, but for now I loved letting him guide me.

Soon he started to tremble and tense up like I did, letting go of my hair and taking my place by putting his own fist around the base of his cock. "Do you want to watch me come?" he growled, his rough hold on himself surprising me. I'm sure he could see how amazed I was as I nodded mutely. A couple of vigorous strokes and his hips thrust forward as hot liquid exploded out of him, making ropey patterns on his chest.

For the life of me I can't tell you why, but that made me so hot I kind of wanted to touch myself while I lay next to him.

This uninhibited bitch inside me had appeared from nowhere, and, wow, was she fun! When he calmed down, the expression on his face was content but not the least bit tired. He didn't miss my squirming and rubbing up against him, and soon had me propped up on pillows, watching me while I watched myself masturbate for him in the mirror over the bed. With him, everything and anything seemed normal. Lucky me!

It went on like that all night, mixed in with a shower and room service, a burger for him and a bento box for me. "Do you think the day will ever come when we can be in the same room and NOT touch each other?" I asked him. He just laughed.

In the morning we were back in the sunken tub, eating waffles and watching the sun come up. I know. Perfect, right?

Chapter Fifteen

Anne

PERFECT UNTIL WE got to the parking lot. Some douchebag keyed the doors and sliced the tires of Owen's beautiful truck. We walked around a bit, looking to see if anyone else's car was messed up, but it was just Owen's. Hoping to lighten the moment, I elbowed him in the ribs and quipped, "Hey, did you send somebody the wrong sex toys? Or otherwise piss somebody off?"

He shrugged, disgusted by the stupidity of it all. "Prob'ly just some damn kids." He called the cops and the tow service. I listened to him talk a rental car company into dropping a car off here, and marveled at how professional and persuasive he was, thankful again he was working with our company. But also wondering where he picked up these grown-up, super-suave skills.

He kept looking at his phone and cursing under his breath, because apparently he was supposed to be somewhere. While we waited, I remembered when someone broke into the trunk of my car and thought of the somebody that *I* pissed off—Wyatt. (Sending someone to jail tends to piss them off.)

Was it a coincidence? The tow truck came and flat-bedded

the pickup, and I sat in the rental car while Owen talked to the police. Before he got in the car, he came around to my side and kissed me, smoothing my hair away from my face. Every time we kiss, he seems to get even better at it. My thoughts of conspiracy and evil intent evaporated into the atmosphere, his kisses escalating when he dropped me off at my house. "I have to go back to my place before I go to the office. See you later?"

"Oh absolutely," I murmured, my voice low.

But the minute he drove away, I got in my car and followed him. He knew I had a class, but of course didn't know I was skipping it, because I was determined to finally find out where he lived and why he was so intent on being there. Dialing Ariana on the hands-free at a light, I got voice mail. It was broad daylight, and I was able to keep up with Owen, though he was driving pretty fast. I had the windows open, my hair up in a clip, the wind keeping me from passing out from how flushed and anxious I was. *Where are you going in such a rush, my beautiful, wonderful man? What is the big goddamn secret here?*

Maybe I thought I had the right to know now…because we were, like, intimate, you know? Maybe I just couldn't stand it anymore, seeing him look at his phone and say goodbye all the time. You can't tell me that's not sooooo shady, am I right? It just *is*.

But what I'm doing was even shadier. Ohmygod, this was wrong, stalking him like this. Good people didn't do it, and I'm a good person. This was a boundary I never, ever thought I would cross. He gave a post office box for a mailing address when we hired him, mumbling something about looking for a new place, and now he says he's a superintendent with a curfew (WTF?).

What the heck kind of arrangement was that? A building

manager who lived on site and had to be on call at night? Taylor asked a friend of hers, and he said the only time he'd heard of it was for a senior citizen building. Bottom line, I had to know. Even knowing if he caught me doing it, it would be beyond embarrassing, and he would…think I was nuts.

This *was* nuts, so wrong, and I decided to get out of there before I sank to an even lower level of pathetic. Why was I there? What did I think I would see? It wasn't right to spy on him. What he did when he wasn't with me was not my business. I kept the car running and watched him, my foot on the brake. If I didn't put the car in park, maybe I wouldn't feel so shifty. *I'm just stopping for a moment…*I told myself.

He pulled into the driveway of a large suburban home with ramps instead of stairs leading to the front door. There was a big white van parked in front of his rental car and a young woman with sunglasses on the front porch, rocking on a rocking chair.

I looked down at my phone, knowing I should call Ariana again and check in, but I saw there was a new text message. I didn't recognize the number, but it said:

Hope ur new boyfriend thinks u r worth it bitch.

My mouth dried up and I couldn't swallow the lump of fear in my throat. Only one person would send me that text: Wyatt. I felt the terror rising, starting in my stomach and making my arms go numb, feeling the blood draining from my face. My body was paralyzed but my leg, pressing stupidly hard on the brake, started to shake.

He sent me a text. He knows about Owen, the hotel. He was there, he messed up Owen's truck. My mind went back to my purse, its contents scattered around the trunk after it was broken into. My phone. He put some spyware bullshit on my phone. That's why it had been heating up and running out of juice. He knew everywhere I went and everyone I called.

Then it got worse. When I looked up, Owen sat down next to the girl in the rocker and gave her a kiss and a big hug. She rose, took his arm, and he walked her inside the house, strolling along like a couple who'd been together for years. There was a lot of affection and familiarity there, and on top of my fear, now I felt sick from being lied to. *After a nice fuck with little Annie, he's ready to get back to his real girlfriend...wife?*

"Answer," I commanded the hands-free, my response running on auto-pilot when Ariana called me back.

"Anne, how was it! Where are you?"

"I'm sitting in my car outside Owen's house, I followed him and he just kissed a pretty girl and walked her inside." My voice sounded tinny, like mechanical voice mail.

"Oh, my God, Anne, for fuck's sake! I'm so sorry, uh, shit!" I could tell she was having a panic attack, her voice breathless. "Listen, we'll talk later about this, but I have something to tell you."

The back door of my Prius opened and closed. I felt something hard and cold, something metal pushed against my neck. A gun? A man's arm reached around and pressed the red button on the hands free, ending the call. Of course Ariana called back immediately, the Bluetooth buzzing. All I had to do was say "Answer."

"Don't fucking answer that, Anne. I love you so much, I don't want to shoot you." Wyatt pressed the cold muzzle of the gun against me, his mouth on the back of my neck, his left hand cupping my face. The phone kept buzzing. "I know you weren't seeing other men for a long time, Anne, you've been waiting for me. I've been watching you. The timing wasn't right yet, we both knew it, we both had to rethink what happened." When he started stroking my cheek with his thumb, my trembling became outright shaking. I wanted to say something, something brave like the cops on *Law and Order*, but absolutely nothing came out of my mouth.

"I knew that guy you hired was trouble the minute you hired him. I could tell by the way he looked at you. You couldn't help it, because you're so innocent." I closed my eyes, trying to get myself together, but instead imagined Wyatt watching me from a rooftop, taking pictures of me.

Reaching down the front of my shirt, he thumbed open the front-close on my bra, pushing it aside far enough that he could surround my breast with his hand and flick the nipple. "Ooooh, fuck, you don't know how long I've wanted to touch you." I felt his hot breath on my neck. "I'm going to punish you for spending the night with him, but that's nothing compared to what I'm going to do to him and his other girlfriend."

When I felt the gun droop in his hand, I went for it. My foot went from the brake to punching the gas as hard as I could, and the car sped across the street, bounced up the curb and ran into a tree in Owen's front yard. The last thing I remember is the blare of the car horn, a loud bang, and my cheek resting on the airbag. There was white powder in the air. Then nothing.

Chapter Sixteen

Owen

ANNE FINALLY OPENED her eyes, doing that shifty-eyed, blinking thing people do when they don't know where they are. "You're in the hospital, and the police have Wyatt," I said, "You're okay, had the wind knocked out of you. You've been in and out, you kept passing out."

Her mom came in, and I stepped back while they hugged and cried, whispering "My sweetheart," "It's okay," and other phrases I still wish I could hear from my own mom. Ariana joined in next, and more tears and hugs of joy celebrated the knowledge we shared that this could have ended so much differently.

Susan had filled me in on what Wyatt'd done to Anne the first time around. Fucking insane prick. When Anne closed her eyes again, Susan came over to me and gave me a kiss on the cheek. "I owe you everything, Owen. Come over here and give us the whole story, blow by blow, I haven't heard the whole thing myself yet."

"I was on the porch, and when I went inside with my sister, the next thing I heard..."

"Your sister? That was your sister?" Anne bleated, turning her face into the pillow.

It suddenly occurred to me what Anne saw and what she must've *thought* she was seeing. "You followed me, and you thought I was with another woman? You thought that's what I was hiding when I had to leave all the time?" I threw back my head and roared, not wanting to mock her, but letting my relief fly out in big gusts of laughter.

Ariana's arms crossed and she squinted at me. "I don't get it. Why do you have to live there like that with your sister?"

All those blue eyes on me. Confession time. I used to explain this to people often, before I decided not to, so I had the speech down pat. "My parents died ten years ago in a car crash. That left me to take care of my sister like they had done her whole life. I was sixteen, she was twenty. Her name is Laura, and she has Down syndrome. When she turned twenty-eight, I realized that she needed more than I could give her by myself, so I formed a nonprofit and created Ability House, a group home for Downs and other specially-abled young adults. Part of the charter is that someone has to be there at all times, 24/7, in case something goes wrong. That's why I sleep there."

"Why didn't you just tell me? Why did you have to keep it a big mystery?!" Anne's voice was full of pain, but also guilt.

"Because of the way you're looking at me right now. You all have your damn pity-faces on, thinking 'Oh, look at that poor young man, all the things he has to give up for his sister.'"

They looked away, because it was absolutely true. "I got tired of the pity-faces, and everyone feeling sorry for me. The people who live in that house are great, and they give out more love than the rest of the world combined. That's why I don't tell people. That's why I was scared to be involved with you, Anne. The situation is so hard to explain."

Everyone else seemed frozen in place, so I took charge. "Ariana and Susan, why don't you sit in those chairs and relax?" They followed my instructions, and I sat on the bed, holding Anne's hand. She was crying, just short of sobbing, obviously feeling bad about jumping to conclusions. "There's no way you could've known, Anne. It was time for me to tell you anyway. I was going to."

Now Ariana's shoulders shook while she buried her face in her hands. "I saw him last night, I saw Wyatt watching you, sitting in the stands. I didn't want to..." She looked over at their mother. "I didn't want to spoil your evening with Owen. I knew you'd be freaked, so I decided I would tell you today. But you could've been *killed*, the fucking bastard could've *killed* you because I didn't saa-haay anythiiiing!!!" She kept her head down, wiping tears and snot on her sleeve. "Liz was checking into getting a restraining order."

Susan put her arms around Ariana, rubbing circles into her back the way moms do. It's not the first time I've gotten that ache of missing my mom around Susan. She'd visited the office a few times, bringing food or something they forgot to bring from home.

"So. I went inside with my sister, and caught up with the house mother on duty, getting a grocery list together, and all of a sudden we heard a loud crash and a car horn. I see a guy hauling ass halfway down the street and, more importantly, Anne passed out over the air bag. Called 911, they sent an ambulance, and the cops picked the guy up later at his parents' house, the idiot. He's back in jail, and Anne won't even have to testify in court. They'll record her testimony but the police say he already admitted everything. Bye, bye, asshole!"

Taylor came in and rushed into Anne's arms, followed by more hugging, kissing and crying.

"What are you doing here?" Susan asked. "Did somebody call you?"

"Well yeah, Ariana texted me but…I was already here. As a matter of fact, can you, uh, come with me in a couple minutes and help me with something?" She sat next to Anne, talking for a while, then gave her another hug. Mom and Taylor left, vowing to return within the hour.

Anne filled me in on the dirty details of what happened in her car right before the accident, what he did (touch her!) and what he said (I love you!). Ariana was crying again. I had to turn away and punch a chair cushion, my vision seared blinding white with rage.

I took about twenty deep breaths, finally understanding why the angry assholes I know do the stupid things they do. It sucks to feel this way, like you want to kill someone. I'm not an angry guy, and haven't experienced it since my parents were killed by that drunk driver. But I went to the drunk driver's court hearing, and they gave him two years. There again, blinding anger. And I won't even talk about what I felt when he got out after a year for "good behavior." One stinking year in jail after killing my parents!

Returning to the present and calming myself, I asked Anne "What made you think of doing that, driving the car onto the lawn into a tree?"

We had a good laugh when she said "I saw it on *Law and Order*. The woman drove the car off the road into a tree and got away."

And then it was past time for me to leave again, because everyone at Ability House was pretty upset.

Anne told me later it took hours before she could even tell Ariana about our wonderful night, it was so unbelievable and unlike her former self. When she described her bold moves to her sister, Anne said it reminded her of cramming for an exam.

Ariana's comment was, "I guess you were making up for lost time!"

I realized that at some point Anne and I would have to talk about the post-nooky recap, what should and shouldn't be shared with her sister. On the other hand, as long as it didn't have a hashtag, it wasn't so bad.

Susan

In a building behind the hospital, Taylor and I entered a small lounge where a counselor in a white jacket waited. Embroidered on her jacket were the words Las Vegas Hospice Center. When I read that, I stepped back, hand to my chest, gasping. "Hospice! It's too soon for hospice!"

Taylor put her arms around me and helped me to a chair, tears glistening in her eyes while she gestured wordlessly at the counselor, as if to say, "Listen."

"While everyone's case is different," the counselor said, "Tina is exhibiting some of the signs of end-stage metastatic breast cancer. Taylor tells me that imaging shows Tina has both brain and liver metastases, is that right?"

I nodded, rubbing my palms up and down my thighs vigorously, hoping rubbing would remind me this wasn't a nightmare.

"Taylor also tells me Tina's been acting childlike, anxious and depressed. Plus, she's had a few falls, and is having difficulty hearing. This is all true, right, Susan?"

I stood and started pacing around the room. Taylor had arranged for the home health aide to stay with Tina, but she sat slumped over a table, head in hands. I leaned forward as if

I were listening to an important lecture, mentally taking notes, trying to be the logical one.

"The thing to do now," the counselor continued, "is to decide if and at what point Tina should come here to our facility. Things will start to happen more and more quickly, there will be more pain, swelling in the belly and the legs, confusion and nausea."

"But shouldn't she stay home, where it's familiar?" I wailed, my hands shaking.

Taylor turned to me, still a ball of misery, but looking in my face. "She won't know, Mama Susan. She sometimes doesn't know now."

The counselor folded her hands. "So that is your decision. When. Most people know when it's time. We can do a better job with many things here, especially pain management. Just let us know when you're ready."

Taylor and I decided not to tell the twins about this until we had to.

Chapter Seventeen

Ariana

A FEW DAYS after the Wyatt incident, my car blew a heat pump, and Javier picked me up at the warehouse. He started shopping the warehouse, dumping about a thousand dollars' worth of random stuff into a bag he grabbed in my office. I put it all back and printed out a list of our best sellers. "Let me pick out the crème de la crème for you, sexy man." I winked and added, "I'll only take the things that I've personally tested."

When we got back to his place we went directly to his bedroom and he dumped the packages on the bed. "So…show me your toys, pretty girl."

He propped some pillows against the headboard and stretched out on the bed lazily, that hot, lean body of his waiting for me to give him a show. The dark, sexy look in his eyes told me he was as into this as I was. He was playing it just right, fascinated but not creepy. My thong was already soaked so I pulled it off…and everything else.

I cupped my breasts in my hands and presented them to him, brushing the nipples with my thumbs. "These are two of my favorite toys. Do you like them?" My voice was barely recognizable, breathy and low.

Sitting up straighter, he licked his lips. "I get so...do you realize that's, like, your sex voice, the way you sound right now? Damn, it just wrecks me..."

He pulled me onto his lap, my tits inches from his face. "And, oh, yes, I like them very much. Show me how you play with them." I couldn't resist that pushy tone he uses, so I did what he said, twisting and pulling my nipples, sending a bolt of arousal shooting straight to my sex. I felt my skin heat with embarrassment, but somehow I wasn't rattled enough to stop.

"I'll bet you have lots of toys in there." He stretched over and opened the bag, rummaging around. "Ohh, look at this!" He emptied a bunch of vibrators onto the bed, a beautiful dildo, and a butt plug and, of course, lubricant. "You filthy girl, mmm, I'm going to undo my pants now, because I'm thinking about you playing with these toys." He gazed at me with heavy-lidded eyes. "So who's in charge here?"

"We both are."

"Why...uh..." He swallowed, temporarily incoherent. It's kind of funny how distracted he is when I'm naked, how the smooth operator gets all speechless. Which was just fine, because I was going to talk dirty enough for both of us.

He examined a giant black vibrating penis and a sculptural bright yellow thing with vibrators on each end, turning them on and off, holding them up to his cheek and pressing them against...ahem...other parts of his body and mine. I'd already decided it's because he's so confident in his hotness that he can be totally uninhibited. He seemed to be having a grand old time, but never took his eyes off me.

I raised one gadget high, a mysterious-looking thing with a leopard print and a jewel instead of a button. "Now this, this is something completely new. Gotta say I kind of want to be in a relationship with this toy!"

Pressing the jewel, I climbed onto his lap and held the rumbly gadget to his cheek. He pulled away, startled. "Feels completely different, right? It's called the Womanizer and it doesn't vibrate, it sucks!" He tilted his head, looking confused. "It sucks on my clit, dude! I can go from zero to yowza in less than a minute!"

"A minute? Seriously?!" Holding the device against my nipple, he said in a heated voice "I'll be wanting a demo of that, but does it work here too?"

"Oh, crap!" I cried, squirming and finally pushing the thing away. "I hadn't tried that yet, dear God!" My nipple was sticking out about as far as it possibly ever, ever could, and I was already close to orgasm, suddenly aware of that clutching feeling between my legs. His nostrils flared while he used it on the other nipple, lighter this time. It was somehow more effective that way, and I shuddered, flushing and trembling.

"When you use it, you know, down there, I go off like a rocket. What do you want to watch, my pussy or my face?"

He smirked. "How about both? Can we do it twice?"

"Noooo! It's too embarrassing!"

"Okay then, your face."

"Good answer, pervert." I lay back on the pillows. He snuggled up next to me, the hand with the toy between my legs. "Okay, go!"

Javier

I used to like sweet girls, watching them blush, enjoying their surprise when I knew how to turn them on. But Ariana…damn! She is the best of both worlds.

One minute she'd be bold and fearless, kind of challenging me, like with the Womanizer, and filling my head with dirty possibilities.

Then she'll take a step back, kind of funny and adorable like the twenty-two-year-old girl she actually is. She makes me want to blow her mind, and, looking at this tiny vibrator thing...I'm ready.

"Tell me when it's in the right place," I said. But it was just like she said it would be. I pressed the button and she closed her eyes, her belly tightening, *everything* tightening while she clawed at the sheets beneath her.

"AhhahhAhhahh" she cried out, her voice getting higher, face scrunched up into a trembling mask, hips tipping up. "EH!" It was like an electric shock went through her, she trembled and came so violently. I took the thing away and trailed some kisses up her neck to her mouth until her body began to relax and she opened her eyes.

"Wow." I stroked her forehead. "That looked intense. How did it feel?"

"I'm so embarrassed that you saw my O-face like that. I must look so weird, but...it is what it is." She stretched out again and held my face in her hands. "It's different, it feels very focused on that one area. We get so many emails from women who have never *had* an orgasm before they used this, so that's great. But it's not...it's just not real, like with you. Your voice, the scruff of your beard, your man-fingers, not to mention your tongue and your lips. Oh, man, I'm getting wet again just talking about you! Anyway, coming with this is like low fat ice cream and turkey bacon, good but it's just not the same for me."

Okay, now I felt like a fucking god! She was so honest and funny, I wanted to say...but instead I said, "So, do you think I'm like, a national treasure?! Maybe you could clone me and sell me on your site?" She fake-slapped my arm and draped those endless legs of hers over my hips. I managed to keep talking. "But ya' know, that Womanizer thing kinda scares me. Imagine when every woman in the world finds out she can get herself off in less than a minute with that thing!"

Leaning her head on one hand, lazily applying the Womanizer to various parts of our bodies, she had a thoughtful look on her face. "I see where you're going with this," she said. "A woman can go to a sperm bank and pick out a nice, intelligent daddy for her baby, so we don't need an actual man for that anymore. I've also heard they're going to be able to form sperm from women's stem cells soon, so two women will actually be able to create a child with both sets of genes. I can reach out to the world via internet and make a great living, so I don't need a physically strong man to kill animals for me or bring in crops anymore."

"That's right," I agreed. "I think you ladies are going to start phasing out the male gender soon, because we know you're smarter and more intuitive than men. You don't need us anymore!"

"Huh! A new and improved world! No war, no *Beavis and Butt-head*, no leaving the toilet seat up!" She started tickling my balls and lightly running her hand up and down my cock, which was of course, growing.

"Yeah, but no Shakespeare, no iPhone, no...Stan Lee?" My voice sounded tight, even to me.

"Hmmm. Sooooo, I think the bottom line is boredom. Women have to keep you guys around to avoid boredom." She was *licking* me now, no joke, the crook of my elbow, my neck, the barbell on my nipple and...lower. And suddenly she got up and just walked away! "Sorry. Gotta pee." She was chuckling to herself, knowing that everything she just licked was cold now, really missing her.

I was ready for her when she came back. There was a mysterious stretchy black round thing in its own little suitcase. I'd flicked it on when she was in the bathroom and already knew how strong it was, but I pretended I didn't. "So what about this thing?" I asked.

"Ohhh, reviews say that thing will do a tango on your tool, try it out! It's a high-tech cock ring, the Tor, and it's even rechargeable. I've always wanted to use it on someone." She stretched it over me, all the way back, with the wider part behind my balls. Watching her was so funny, she was literally like a kid playing with a new toy. "When you position it this way, it vibrates your nads." She pressed a button on the side.

"Whoa," I said, "Everything, it vibrates everything!" I kissed her and pulled her on top of me. "I want you to feel it too."

"The old-timers tell me you used to have to plug this shit in to get a good vibration, but no more." She turned the wide part so it was on top now, and I saw her evil plan. She relaxed herself and sank down on my cock, breathing deeply until the vibrating section was against her clit. "This is supposed to cause a multiple speedgasm for both of us in minutes, maybe seconds. I think of it as a guybrator, the best toy for boys."

I felt a pressure building in my core from the strong vibe, and I couldn't stop staring and thrusting into her from below while she met me, stroke for stroke. Her legs started to shake, her sexy cries higher and louder. She drew me in tighter and gasped, "I'm close, ohohh!" just in time for me to follow her over in a toe-curling, mind-blowing orgasm that went on for...okay, I didn't look at my watch.

"Damn." Her swollen lips called to me, and I pulled her in, raining kisses on her face and neck too. "Speedgasm, for sure!" I reached down and pulled the thing off and she pressed the button to turn it off. Suddenly it hit me. "Hey, uh…we didn't use a condom."

She gasped and put her hands to her cheeks. "Oh my God!"

I started to have a sick feeling in my stomach when she ran her fingers through my hair. "Psych! I'm on birth control, have been for a while!" she whispered. "You said you were just tested, so I went, too. All good."

I felt my whole body relax…possibly too much. After more kissing and touching, I heard this come out of my mouth. "Did I, uh, tell you I was engaged once?"

Shaking her head, she snuggled up close to me, making no demand for me to continue unless I wanted to. I threaded my fingers thru those red waves of hair. "She…totally kicked the shit out of me. We were young, I loved Gina, I loved her family, and I never saw it coming. We were getting ready for work, she was in the shower, and her phone buzzed. It was a message, 'Tomrw @3, Heartland Motel?'"

Ariana turned toward me and buried her face in my neck, holding me tight.

"I borrowed a friend's car she wouldn't recognize and waited in the parking lot. It was a guy from her work. I took pictures of them kissing before they keyed into the room, and again when they left. When I confronted her, she was all, 'Oh, I don't know what I was thinking, I'm so sorry!' I was numb at first, out of touch for a few days, but she knew it was over and gave me the ring back."

The sun was shining through a window, warming my face. I felt better somehow, sharing this horrible fucking story with her.

"Her family thought I was nuts, that there was no way she would do that, so I was glad I took the pictures. I was close with one of her brothers, and I cared what he thought, so I showed him the shots of the two of them kissing in the parking lot of the motel. Of course we don't hang out anymore, but I still wanted him to know the truth."

Ariana held me, stroking my face. "It's funny, you and I had the same reaction to having our hearts broken," she said. "We both decided either every person on earth's a cheater, or they'll leave or disappear. We both thought we would play around and leave them before they leave us, right?"

"Let's call a time-out on that strategy for now, can we?" *Fuck! Ariana's totally got my number on that.* "It's interesting, though, guys are usually the ones who want revenge, and you're the one who wants to screw with Sanjay, tell his girlfriend the truth. I spent a long time wondering what I did wrong, which I've heard is usually what women do."

Before today, I had only told my mother and Daniella that story about my engagement. Just thinking about it made me tired. I stretched my arms back around Ariana. "Let's take a little nap."

I set my phone for forty-five minutes, and we slept curled around each other like puppies. I could get used to this. I was leaving for Mexico soon, and wished she could come with me, but I knew she had final exams.

Chapter Eighteen

Anne

ARIANA, JAVIER, AND I were totally impressed by our tour of the place where Owen's sister lived, Ability House. It was absolutely spotless, and so nice, providing a comfortable home for Laura and seven other people in their twenties. There were posters around the house reminding everyone of their chores—cooking, shopping, and laundry. There was a schedule of trips to the YMCA, concerts, haircuts, doctors, the library, and church. Paid and volunteer staff also took them to work and to classes for computer and reading skills.

"We run it as a nonprofit, with bylaws and board members, many of whom were my parents' friends." Owen had a lot to be proud of, and I could understand now why he had to be available if something happened.

"I'm sorry. Again," I said quietly to him. "I can see there are a lot of moving parts to this place, and you have to stay on top of them."

When Owen introduced me to his sister Laura, he said "This is my girlfriend, Anne." His girlfriend! That sounded wonderful to me. Wyatt used to avoid any kind of a label, just using my name. I could've been some random woman he picked up by the side of the road. And now I could see the difference. When Owen introduced me as his girlfriend, it meant he considered our relationship serious.

I could see Laura was checking me and Ariana out, but the more we talked, the more we liked each other. She admired the French braid in my hair, and it only took a few minutes for me to braid her hair in a similar style. She loved it! We went up to her room, and Ariana fussed over her makeup and we had some laughs together. When I told her I was a business major, she told me about a personal finance class she took, and we discussed different kinds of software.

Owen watched carefully, taking it all in. That made sense, considering the only family they had was each other. "By the way," he said, "you guys have something else in common— graduation. Laura is graduating from high school with a real diploma this weekend. Last time, she got an alternative degree, but she decided to take regular, mainstream high school classes two years ago, and here we are!"

"Would you like to come to my graduation, Anne?" she asked shyly. "They asked me to give a little speech!"

Keeping my face neutral, I looked at Owen. I didn't want to horn in on a family event, but he immediately nodded and smiled. "Whaddya say, Anne? We have one other ticket. You're welcome to join us."

"Oh my gosh, yes! I'm honored."

Laura lowered her voice and said "I know it's because I have Downs. They want me to give the 'If I can do it, you can do it' speech." She gave me a sly smile. "But luckily, I actually *can* do it!"

We hung out while Owen and Javier looked around the garage and worked on ideas for the transportation stuff. I signed up to volunteer on Sundays to drive people around. After exams, I could spend even more time here.

Javier

Owen was showing me around the yard and the garage and said, "I feel like you were kind of eyeballing me weirdly just now. What's up?"

It was true. I had been wondering about some things. "I looked online where nonprofits have to list their income and expenses," I said. "This place costs a fortune to run. How do you do it?"

"My parents owned a business, and they were good investors. When they died, I sold the business and inherited the whole estate. So... does that make you think less of me?"

"What?"

"That my parents were wealthy, and I don't have to deal with where the money will come from?"

"Hey, money makes things easier, for sure. It's easier to keep your eye on the big picture when you don't have to wonder where your next meal is coming from, or your family's next meal."

Owen asked for some advice about keeping the Ability House vehicles maintained, and I gave him some suggestions. But I had one more money-related question.

"So here's the next logical question, rich guy," I said. "Why did you get a part-time job working for two college girls?"

Owen ducked a little, obviously embarrassed. "Living here, I don't get to meet people my age. I was looking through the campus newspaper for stuff to do, concerts, whatever, and I saw their ad for a business manager. I went to their website and, uh…"

We both laughed, knowing what he was thinking the minute he saw their picture. "Say no more, I get it," I said. "I didn't want anything to do with my sister's boyfriend's sister…until I met her." I shrugged. "And that was that."

Later, I said to him, "I was thinking about what you said, about how people think if you have a few bucks, life is easy. Growing up, I didn't have to worry about every penny either. Even though my dad's a jerk who takes advantage of vulnerable women, he did keep a roof over our heads and pretty much show up most of the time."

I was surprised to hear those words come out of my mouth. My dad was the biggest player around, and I was ashamed of that, but not exactly an angel myself.

"But you, Owen, I feel like…you appreciate your advantage, you're not the spoiled rich guy. What you've done with the group home is pretty cool. You could be spending that money on hookers and weed candy. I mean, you do live near Las Vegas!"

I could see he'd never even heard of weed candy, and that was good. It occurred to me Owen and I have that other thing in common, always having to carry an emotional weight on our shoulders, having had to grow up fast. His response was to be conservative, dorky. Mine was to attempt to kick the world's ass…until I figured out it wasn't going to work.

"On the other hand," I said, slapping him on the back, "I do think you need a new, fun ride other than your pickup truck and that ugly white van. What can I pick up for you when I'm in Mexico, rich guy?" I was driven both by the desire for profit and to put some fun in the life of this philanthropic knight in shining armor.

He thought a minute and his face brightened. "Can you get me one of those VW hippie vans? We need something for smaller trips, like for four people, because the big van is a real gas guzzler."

"God, you are a complete dork! I was thinkin' sports car, but a hippie van?"

"Yeah, yeah!" Now he was getting excited. "Maybe one where we could raise the roof, or pull down a bed, you know, like, one with peace signs all over it. I'm seeing myself rolling up to the soccer game with that!"

"That's called the Samba van, and they were actually made in Brazil. But sure, I can get that for you, rich guy!" I could barely choke the words out, I was laughing so hard. Knowing Ariana's love for variety, I added "That bed is a good idea. Maybe I'll borrow the van sometime."

Chapter Nineteen

Anne

ARIANA WENT HOME with Javier, and Owen had somewhere he wanted to take me, but on the way there I had a confession to make. "I uh, have to tell you, I thought...oh, this is horrible. I thought because they have similarities, people with Downs, I thought they were..."

Interrupting, he gave my shoulder a quick squeeze. "You thought they were all retarded, all the same intellectually. I know, it's okay. A lot of people do. But there are ranges of IQ within the syndrome, Laura's IQ is above eighty, just slightly below regular adult average. And we don't know what they're capable of. Downs kids used to only live until they were about twenty-five, because they were put in institutions. Now the average lifespan is sixty. But there are some who aren't like Laura and need to live in a more sheltered environment their whole lives."

"It's not okay!" I slapped my thigh, pissed at myself. "It's like racism, lumping people together like that. She's so smart, with such a great sense of humor. I feel ashamed."

Owen reached over and took my hand. "It's good you feel that way but, on the other hand, you can't know everything about everything." His voice was soft when he added, "It's weird, though. I feel, like…I feel lighter, just because you know about Laura and you haven't run the other way. Yet."

We pulled up in front of a big old factory that was being converted into loft apartments. The building was about a mile from the SNU campus, and a few blocks from the Two Much warehouse. "These are going to be so nice," I said, looking at the billboard advertising the fancy condos. "Are you thinking about buying one?" He nodded, smiling while we walked inside. I had been wanting to ask him if he'd ever thought about *not* living full time at Ability House. Was it even possible? Was it a money thing?

The elevator took us to the top, and we walked out onto a roof terrace. We could see for miles, enjoying the view of the mountains that surround Las Vegas. The long, lean shell of a pool was propped up on a wooden frame, and building and landscape materials were piled up everywhere. "Wow, they're building a pool up here, amazing. Looks expensive."

There was a lovely desert breeze blowing, and I remembered the sexy panties I had on under my skirt. Ariana took me shopping and got me to give up my comfy almost-granny panties. I was hoping to show the new ones off to an audience of one.

He shrugged and took my hand again. "Let's check out a unit. One of them is almost done." I didn't stop to wonder why he seemed so familiar with the staircases and the locks. The finished unit was not huge, but it was absolutely breathtaking, with floor to ceiling windows like a movie star home in a magazine. It also had a modern kitchen with gleaming appliances, and an island with barstools took up one end of the room, with a sectional couch in a bright abstract print dominating the other side.

There was a long table with six chairs. On it, a big glass vase with a giant bouquet of white jasmine flowers released my favorite scent into the air. Owen pulled me close and pressed his forehead to mine. "Do you like the flowers?" he asked, his voice low and seductive.

"I'm so…I'm confused." He kissed me softly, and I melted into him, talking quietly in his ear so my words wouldn't get lost in the high ceiling. "I wanted to ask if you would always live at Ability House, but I didn't…I didn't feel I had the right to. Is this apartment yours, are you going to rent it? Is that why you have my favorite flowers here?"

His lips brushed my fingertips and kissed my neck, my cheeks, my eyelids. "I never had a reason not to live there. Until now. I *could* live here, I interviewed somebody to be the night supervisor at the house, but only if you would live here with me."

He'd seemed so sure of himself at first, but then he paused. "I mean, uh, not right away, if you don't feel ready yet. But I bought this building after I met you. I told myself it was an investment but…every step of the way, I saw myself living here with you." He was holding me tighter now, kissing the top of my head and clutching my butt and my back, as if he was afraid I would run away.

"Bought the building? This building, you…own it?!" I pulled away from him and felt…cold. The truth was, I never, ever wanted to be out of the warmth of his arms but we *had* to talk! I pulled a chair out from the table, and patted the seat for him to sit in it. "You sit here, and I'll sit across from you. We will not touch each other, and we will talk, get all our secrets out on the table, okay?"

Owen chuckled and rapped on the table with his knuckles. "Out on the table, ooo*kay!*"

Elbow on the table, chin resting on my hand, I narrowed

my eyes at him. "Are you making fun of me? 'Cause it's not fair, since you got to see my secret in a goddamn police report! And there were *pictures*, for gosh sake! I just had to…fill in the details."

Reaching across the table, he took my hand in his and kissed it. "You're right. I'll be brave like you and reveal all."

I pulled my hand away. "Okay, but no touching. You are apparently someone completely different from the Owen Reeves guy who works in our office. Who are you, really, and what's the deal, here?"

Sitting straight up in the chair, his arms crossed over his chest, Owen said, "So, uh…I told you my parents died in a car accident ten years ago, when I was sixteen, and a few years later Laura moved into Ability House, and I moved into the attic apartment to supervise and take over the night shift while I got my degree at SNU." He cleared his throat, squirming in his chair. "The fact is that…I built Ability House with the money from my parent's estate. Which is, uh…*my* money. My parents were investors and business owners, and I inherited their estate."

"So you own Ability House, and this building, this condo…or whatever you call it. You…*own* it."

"Well, Ability House is a nonprofit with a board of directors and…"

"Okay, fine," I interrupted, "but it was built with your money, right? And you own this building?" I heard myself saying these things, trying to reconcile Mr. Monopoly here with Owen-who-works-in-our-warehouse.

"Yeah. And, just, uh…while we're getting it out there, I also own the warehouse you're renting for Two Much."

Laughing, I said, "So that's why the rent is so cheap! You've been giving us a deal, is that right Mr. Monopoly?! Do you own Park Place and Boardwalk, too?" He blushed, and I couldn't stop cackling. It was just too ridiculous! When I realized he was Daddy Big Bucks, and he was working part-time for us for about $25 an hour, I tried to ask him why, but I was doubled over, choking with laughter.

Suddenly I was swept out of the chair by a pair of strong arms, staring up as the vaulted ceiling went by in a blur. Striding along like he was carrying a small child, he growled "I'm calling off the no-touching rule and showing you the bedroom. Is that okay, Miss Annie?"

Owen's wonderful face was so close to mine, I had to kiss him. I tried giving him a little peck on the lips, but he wasn't having it, giving me a deeper kiss that promised more.

"Owen, I hope you have a bed in there. Do you?" My answer bounced up to meet me when he dumped me on a lovely king-size bed and stood staring at me, his hands on his hips. God, he was so gorgeous, his big shoulders and narrow hips. His shirt fit like it was made for him, revealing every muscle. And his jeans, uh, seemed to be getting tighter by the moment.

He was watching me watching him, his eyes twinkling. "What are you looking at, dirty girl?" I felt a shiver, an excited shiver. Should I be less excited this time? I mean, I know what's under the jeans now, I know what might happen next, and I know how wonderful it can feel. And I want to feel it, oh, yes I do!

Owen

Anne's a natural. An enthusiastic natural. When she pushed herself up off the bed and stood in front of me, she took my shirt off. I felt a little light-headed from her fragrance when she ran her hands up my arms, across my chest and down my back. "Are you okay with the windows and, you know, no curtains?"

Her smile was devilish. "I actually...kind of like the idea. Is that perverted?"

"Absolutely not, I think all women who look like you should stand naked in front of windows." She must've liked that answer because she pulled me in and pushed her hips against me, a sweet invitation if ever there was one. And when she stepped back and took off her shirt *and* her bra, well...that was more of an order than an invitation.

I wanted to take my time and nuzzle her hair, kiss her neck, but she brought my hands to her breasts. Hissing when I cupped them and my fingers scraped her nipples, she was breathing fast, her eyes half closed. "I love it when you touch me," she said in a husky whisper.

She explored the hair on my chest and followed it down to my belly, tracing her finger across the top of my belt buckle before she put her hand down there and stroked my cock. "Holy shit, Anne, you're getting awfully good at that." My voice cracked, and I jerked a little when she undid my belt, button, and zipper in short order, pulling it all down, kneeling and flicking me with her tongue. I was facing the tall windows, not caring about anything except her red hair below me and the feel of her lips around me, working me over. Her little noises were so hot, like she was...humming, vibrating around me until I knew I was almost there.

When I lifted her off and pulled her onto the bed with me, she was pouting, her lips red and swollen. "Hey, I was just getting a feel for that."

"You definitely were, but I don't want to come that way

right now. Let me have my fun now." Kissing her until she was soft and dreamy, lying against the pillows again, I had to lean back and look at her, her hair so pretty against her creamy white skin. "You are so beautiful. When I saw you wore a skirt today, I was having a hard time putting words together wondering what was under there."

I ran my fingers up her thigh and lifted the skirt, surprised by a bright pink, lacy pair of panties. "These are nice, but I think…" As I pulled the skirt and panties off, I saw that she was waxed, completely bare except for a neat patch of red hair. "Holy shit, I love your red hair, but this is hot."

She was blushing under her freckles. "I'm…I'm glad you like it. It feels so…different."

I spread her with my hands and just stared—her pussy looked like a glistening pink flower, and I couldn't wait to taste her. I could tell right away it must feel different for her, too, because when I touched her with my thumb and licked her, she started squirming and moaning immediately. "Huh! Huu-uh!" she gasped, flinching but thrusting toward me at the same time. Swollen and hot, her slit was getting very wet as I flattened my tongue, adding pressure while I swiped all along, then twirling my tongue around her clit. She was watching me, propped up on pillows, and able to see everything I was doing. Every once in a while she'd close her eyes and throw her head back.

I picked up the pace a little, flicking and sucking on that hypersensitive knob that made her thrash around on the bed. Wetting a couple of fingers, I crooked them inside her and kept eating her, loving the way her breath hitched and she jerked and trembled to her core. Her noises of pleasure were so hot, when my fingers found the little ridges inside, and I could feel her silky channel swelling and quivering while her whole body bucked intensely.

"Come on my tongue, baby, do it. You're so close." I could hear my voice was tense, because I was close myself, but my words set her free, and she wailed her release, saying my name. *My* name. She made me feel like I could conquer the world, like I was *the man*, at least to her.

"Mmmmm. Laaay here with me," she purred, patting the spot next to her on the bed. I didn't realize I was still kneeling next to the bed, looking at her, until she said it. Her skin was so warm when she flexed into me, and I pulled the blanket over us for a proper cuddle. She arched a brow. "Do I want to know why you're so good at that?"

"Uh...I don't know. Do you?" I couldn't keep my hands off her, stroking, pinching, cradling her breasts, my hands moving up and down her body. I just couldn't help myself. Her skin was like warm velvet, if there is such a thing. "It's funny that we've known each other for more than a year, watched each other carefully. But we're just now getting personal. Are you asking for more about my sexual history?"

She blushed of course and nodded. "Yes, but not right now. You haven't finished making love to me yet, and I can't decide which I like better, you fucking me or you licking my pussy. And judging from your friend, there, bumping me in the belly, I'd say we're ready to settle the question." She put both hands around my dick, pumping me like she meant it. And then she did the most incredible thing.

Springing out of bed and walking over to those tall glass windows, she put her hands flat on them. The light was just right on her naked body, her pale skin, her perfect tits, her curvy hips. She spread her legs and stuck her glorious butt out in my direction, her hair messy and sexy down her back. *Damn.*

Looking over her shoulder at me with a look I hadn't seen

before, she said, "Do I have to come over there and get you?"

I didn't need to hear that twice, and I was on my way to her in a heartbeat. Smoothing my hands up her sides and across her shoulders, I wound her hair around the fingers of one hand, and got a firm grip on her hip with the other. Her head tilted back, and I took her mouth in a hungry kiss, my thighs tight against her behind, my cock resting in paradise between the globes of her ass.

I took a quick look out the window. No obvious freaks staring. "So, my little Red Riding Hood likes to show off, eh? Do you like thinking someone can see us?" Saying that out loud got her going; I'd figured out her kink even before she realized she had it. She groaned and her head rolled farther back and her eyes fluttered closed as she wiggled into me. "You're imagining someone is watching the Big Bad Wolf touch you, aren't you?"

I placed my cock between her legs and rocked back and forth, coating it with her juices, and making sure I slid over her clit with every stroke. *Don't come, don't come, do not come*, I thought to myself, wanting to hang on as long as I could. We were both getting very slick.

"I think I can make you come like this." After a soft moan, she turned to look at me, and there was an unmistakable fever in her eyes. "Tell me, what are you thinking about right now? Are you thinking about my mouth between your legs, or how good my dick feels doing this?"

"Uuumm, both," she panted out. If fooling around in front of a window got her this turned on, so hot she can barely speak, I might be willing to rent a window on Main Street. Leaning into her, I played with both breasts and continued my shallow thrusts. Making fists with her hands on the glass, she whimpered "Uhoh, Aaaahoooh," while her body tensed and she came. I tried to stop moving while she struggled to catch her breath, but continued to pulse a little, so close to coming myself my eyes were closed tight.

"Aren't you going to fuck me now?" she asked in a breathy voice.

The thought of walking away from her warmth was just torture, but I managed to say, "Huh, yeah, uh, condom." Amazingly, she loosened her hand on the glass and handed me the condom she'd been holding there the whole time! *Damn... again!* "Wow, you are...a bad, naughty girl. Are you using me for sex?" Nodding, we grinned at each other, and I had that thing on in a heartbeat. She gasped when I entered her, it was so deep this way. I was still, feeling her adjust around me while I filled her.

For a few minutes that was the total focus of my world, that one small place at her entrance where she gripped me, the plush feel of her inside while she rippled around me. My groin pressed against her edible ass, my hands squeezing and pulling, going faster and harder until I could feel myself getting jagged. "Can you come again?" I choked out. "I'm going to come."

"I'm close, too," she groaned. When she reached a hand down and started shaking, touching herself, I lost it. My orgasm barreled through me, and I cried out, and, thank fuck, she did too. Wow. We clung to each other, exchanging little kisses and laughing at ourselves. When I came back from the bathroom, she lifted the quilt for me to get in and cuddle her again. After I kissed her, she squeezed me and said, "Oh my God, I *love* this. I can't believe how much I like sex! Am I any good at it?"

Her mischievous style just struck me as so funny, I was howling with laughter, and that made her laugh too. "I thought I would pass out when you put your hands on that window! And you had a condom, for godsakes! Let's face it,"

I said, "if you showed up and took your clothes off, that would be enough, but you're a fucking kinkmeister, Little Red, so hot!

"Oh, and you're the big bad wolf, are you?" she pouted, poking me in the chest.

"Yes. Yes, I am," I chuckled, and started tickling her until she rolled away from me, holding her arm out.

"You think I've forgotten, but now I want to know," she said, trying hard to look stern and serious. "Now you have to tell me how you got to be so good at this."

I blew the air out of my lungs, suddenly feeling heavy. "I've been lonely, Anne, so lonely. I've been with more girls than I should. I always felt like, you know, I had to keep it casual because of living with Laura."

She held both my hands under the covers, and whispered "It's okay. Tell me more."

I lay on my back and looked at the ceiling, not wanting her to see my eyes. "Before my parents died, I was a typical teenage guy, good at baseball. I was a pitcher at Summerlin High School."

Excited, Anne sat up and leaned on an elbow, studying me. "Oh, you're *that* Owen Reeves! Now I remember, it was in the paper when I was in, like, sixth grade. You were a big shot, state champs! I didn't even think to Google you! I love baseball, and I played girls' softball until they threw me out in high school. I kind of sucked. So…all the girls reeeeaaaly liked you, the big time pitcher?"

"Uh, yeah, it was kind of like that. One of the seniors gave a party at his parents' house, no parents present, and it was my first time drinking. I was fourteen, a freshman. A senior girl led me into the laundry room and locked the door, sucked my cock until the top of my head blew off. These senior girls kind of passed me around for a while, thought I was sweet.

Sophomore year, I had a girlfriend, but it was one of those things where we were always breaking up, dumb kid stuff. Heading into junior year, I was dating around, playing baseball and fucking like a champ.

"The night my parents were killed by a drunk driver, I was with a friend's big sister, and I don't even remember her name." I heard myself sigh, one of those big what-happened-to-the-last-ten-years sighs. "I'd meet women in class at SNU, and later, after I graduated, I'd meet women in bars, hooking up. It was kind of like that movie *50 First Dates*, no one ever stuck around for very long, you're starting over each time. In the beginning, if I liked someone, I'd try to explain my situation. Looking at the woman's face, I always saw I'd entered the dead zone. Nobody wants to hear that you've got a commitment like that, a serious commitment to care for someone for the rest of your life."

There was a softness in Anne's eyes when she put her hands on the side of my face and kissed me. "There must've been someone...real in all those years. C'mon, Owen, you're too good of a guy for *someone* not to care for you."

Once again, I realized how Anne seems to...see things. She has great instincts about people. I gulped and nodded. "There was a woman three years ago...Heather, a couple of years older. She was an occupational therapist who came to Ability House for a while, to help some people with what they call 'activities of daily living,' mostly typing, brushing your teeth, fixing your hair, getting in and out of cars, that kind of thing. I liked her so much, and hung out with her friends too, mostly couples who were getting married and having kids. After about a year, I thought about asking her to marry me, but she got a job offer back in Boston, where she was from, and just kind of, boom, she was leaving. A kiss on the cheek and see ya! She never even asked if I wanted to keep going. I emailed and called for a while, but she met someone else. I felt kind of...used."

"And recently?" There was a longing in Anne's eyes, a need to know where we were going.

"Shortly after Heather is when I answered the ad in the campus newspaper to work for you. I was telling Javier, I was looking through the paper for ways to meet people and decided to answer your ad." I pressed my lips to her forehead and stroked her hair, chuckling. "Uh, especially after I Googled your company and saw your picture on that funky website you used to have."

"You know what I liked when I first met you at the interview?" Anne said. "I could tell you didn't see me as being part of my sister like a lot of guys do, you saw me as me. And when I get nervous and talk too much, you think it's cute, not annoying." She paused, tracing little circles on my chest. "So, uh, you haven't been, uh, you know, hooking up lately? With women who know more, kind of, what they're doing in the old sackaroo?"

Only Anne could say sackaroo and get away with it. "Honestly, no, not since I met you. I've loved getting to know you and going to soccer, meeting your friends. I also got busy when I bought this building and worked on this apartment, and of course, did my Ability House jobs."

How do I tell her that other women seemed sleazy, and I hoped right from the beginning we'd end up exactly where we are right now? Sounded so sappy. "I like that you're so innocent, but you trust me to do things to you. Raw things. I felt that the first time I met you, that you were...waiting. Waiting to give what you've never given anyone before. I'm so honored that you chose me."

"I chose you because I like your body and your smart yet dirty mind. Of course, now that I know you're Daddy Big

Bucks, I like the way you're not a jerk about it. And I kind of like the rest of you, too." She climbed on top of me, giving me a view of her naked self again, and we started wrestling and tickling and…yeah, *that* happened again. I guess she was making up for lost time. I know I was.

I decided not to push her on the moving-in question. Was it a sad reality that I knew she had to check in with Ariana? I decided that, no, it's a happy reality. I don't have to do and be everything for Anne the way I have for my sister. Anne has good friends, and a great sister, and I feel like…maybe I could even lean on *her* a little.

Still, I added a point that I hoped was in my favor. "Javier is thinking about moving in to the ground floor apartment. I told him we could adapt part of the yard for his dogs, maybe even let them swim in the pool when no one's looking." With a straight face I added "Maybe we should see if Sanjay wants to move in, get the whole gang here." We both had a good laugh at that idea.

Chapter Twenty

Ariana

H ATE ISN'T THE opposite of love. Indifference is.

After our tour of Ability House, Javier sent me this text. "Going to Mexico to buy cars. See you in two weeks."

I mean, sure, he'd mentioned it before. But he went from confessing tortured secrets of his past and texting me three or four times a day to...pretty much nothing. When I texted him "When are you leaving?" he answered "Not sure." I tried to call; he didn't answer. Zilch, zip, nada. Really?

I tried not to freak out. What did it mean? When this happened before, it meant the guy was losing interest. I'd respond the same way and bail out. The ol' *I'll do it to him before he does it to me,* remember? But I *thought* this was different, two players who decided not to play, not to mess with each other's heads. Apparently not.

The first day, I bought a small container of Chunky Monkey and ate it after lunch

The second day, I bought a half gallon of mint chip and ate the whole thing. *Instead* of lunch and dinner.

I've read that guys do this—poof, they drop off the face of

the earth. It's actually *called* poofing, and it supposedly happens because they get too close to you emotionally and it scares them. They go dark while they try to figure it out, and it's somewhat understandable from a fucked-up male standpoint, but frustrating at the same time.

The third day, I had a dinner meeting at Sinatra's Bistro at the Flynn Hotel with a potential vendor. Unfortunately, considering the Sinatra's prices, I was buying. I got there right on time and when I walked through the bar, I saw Javier and an adorable brunette having dinner at a table overlooking the strip.

Stopping briefly to catch my breath, because every ounce of air had been slammed out of my lungs, I saw my vendor four tables back in the other room and numbly made it through my meeting. Javier was gone when I left the restaurant.

Did I text him and ask him WTF?! Did I go directly to his house and pound on his door? I briefly considered sending him a nude photo of myself with a note that said, "This is what you will never touch again," but I didn't.

Instead I bought four bottles of pinot noir, downloaded the six hottest romance novels I could find, and went home and began to read them. I had no classes, and was supposed to be studying for my final exams, so I texted Mom and Anne not to bug me. I caught up with Instagram, Twitter, Facebook and Pinterest, where of course Owen had built zillions of followers and had everything leading buyers to Two Much. A day and a half later, I had a singing visitor.

"Good morning, Mary Sunshine!" Anne proceeded to dance around my room, throwing open the curtains while I covered my head with a pillow. At that moment, I would've rated the bad hangover headache from red wine as 10 on a scale of 10.

I forgot that she had a key. "Do *not* sing the rest of that fucking song!" I croaked, my voice sounding like someone who hasn't talked in a few days. Probably because I hadn't.

Of course, that only egged her on. "Good morning, Mary Sunshine!" she sang, arms wide. "Why did you wake so soooon? You scared the little stars away and you shiiined…aaaaaaway……the mooooon!!!!" She gave it a big-ass high note at the end, just like my mom did when we were little.

Taylor walked in with a bag from McDonalds's, putting it down and clapping madly for Anne's chirpy rendition of the song. "I see the gang's all here," I grumbled. Raising my head and looking at Anne, I snarled "Just because you're finally getting some nookie doesn't mean you can come in here and be so cheerful."

Taylor's mouth fell open and she gasped. "No way! You traded in your V-card? When? With Owen, ohmigawd?! How did it happen?"

I grabbed the bag and fished out a coffee, an orange juice and a nice, greasy breakfast sandwich, chewing and looking from Anne to Taylor. "I don't get it. You didn't tell Taylor? What the hell?" I might be stirring the wrong pot here, but it *was* weird.

Blushing, Taylor laid the rest of the food and drinks out on my dresser. That's Taylor, always serving. "It's not her fault. I've been taking care of my mom, and I'm out of touch."

Clearing her throat, Anne added, "It's not something I could text you about."

We've known each other so long, I could tell there was more to the story. "Taylor, what's up?"

Tears filled Taylor's eyes, and Anne went over and threw an arm around her shoulders.

"I'm so glad to be here," Taylor said. "Could we talk about you guys for a while?"

Okay. I was feeling like shit but, let's face it, when family needs you, nothing else matters. And maybe...maybe I needed to talk, too. I pulled a bottle of cherry vodka out of my closet and poured a generous shot into each cup of orange juice. Bumping our paper cups together, I said, "Here's to sisters drinking before noon!"

"Sisters!"

"Okay, I'll go first," Anne said. "Owen was freaked when I told him I was a virgin, and it was weird at work from then on. Then he showed up Monday at the office with flowers, Chinese food, and twinkling lights on the palm trees behind the office. We talked, checked into a suite at the Mandarin the next night after soccer and..."

Now her face matched our red hair. "It was...intense and wonderful. Candles and sweet words and...we laughed a lot." Tears ran down her cheeks but they were tears of joy. "There was a sunken hot tub overlooking the city," she choked out, sniffing, "just sayin'." When she wiped her tears away, she added, "And he didn't leave before midnight, and he didn't turn into a pumpkin." We laughed at that one, and Taylor and I sighed. Neither of us had a first time like that, but, goddammit, someone should.

When my girls crowded into that funky little room of mine, we each thought we had a secret we couldn't share. Anne was afraid to share, even though it was joy...or maybe because it was joy. She knew Taylor and I were sad, and didn't want to make us feel worse.

"So what about you, Ariana? You said Javier was a player and you could handle it, it was just for fun. You're usually bulletproof, especially with a guy like that." She sat next to me and took my hand. At first I kind of resented her you-should-know-better thing. Among the three of us besties, we don't do slut-shaming, weight-shaming, or otherwise pointing out bad choices. Then she said, "Pretty little lies, huh? We all fall for the same shit. 'You're the only one, you're the best ever, you're special,' right?"

Oh, my God, she totally nailed it! I put my head in my hands and just started sobbing, letting out the hurt I'd been trying to keep inside since I saw Javier in the restaurant. At the end I talked about the damn dogs. "And I miss his dogs, too. I miss petting them and having them jump around on the bed even though they're not supposed to."

"What dogs?" asked Taylor. "He has dogs?" I showed her the pictures on my phone of John, Paul, George, and Ringo, realizing I had individual, group and action shots of the damn dogs like I was their godmother or something.

"I was actually seeing one of Mom's doctors for a while, a resident." Taylor's voice, filled with pain, broke into my thoughts.

Anne and I exchanged glances. "Why is this the first we're hearing about this?"

Pouring herself another shot of vodka, Taylor threw it down the hatch. She already had the flushed, I-don't-give-a-shit glow of plenty of alcohol. "I'm at the hospital or the clinic all the time, who else could I meet? So I met this guy about a month ago, whirlwind relationship, he seemed hardworking, high energy. And that was the problem, my dear friends, that's why you will never meet him. His energy came from an addiction to amphetamines. And how cool—he could write his own prescription! That's why he was arrested while we were out on our third date, in a restaurant near the hospital."

"Wow," Anne said. "That was absolute shit luck." Anne and I exchanged glances, wondering if we hadn't been there for Taylor when she needed us.

"I wish that was my shittiest luck," Taylor said, her breath hitching as she struggled not to cry. She walked over to the window, looking away from us. "After I visited you in the hospital, Anne, your mom and I talked to a hospice counselor. My mom's not going to make it this time. They're saying a couple of months."

And…there it was.

Have you ever heard the phrase "weeping and wailing?" There is such a thing, the gut-wrenching sound that comes out of you when bad news chokes the shit out of you. You hear it, and you wonder who that sound is coming out of. It's you, goddammit. We laid on the bed together, crying and holding hands, for about an hour. Yes, Mama Tina's had the cancer come back three times. But we always believed she'd beat it again.

After a while, I sat next to Taylor and put my arm around her. "Okay, that puts everything in perspective. This is so much more important than men! We don't need men, right?" She gave me a weak smile and nodded. "When's the last time we tried abstinence? It'll be a whole new me. Whaddya say, kid? Let's not be defined by our relationship status."

I sounded so sure of myself, but this void in my gut had knocked me for a loop. How had Javier sneaked up on me like this, opening up parts of me I'd deliberately closed off, or never even knew existed? I thought it was weak to be this heartbroken over an admitted player, and in light of Taylor's news, it was. But feelings are feelings; they're not right or wrong.

Taylor knew this news about her mom would eclipse all the concerns we've ever had. And the big thing here was that a woman who has loved and cared for us our entire lives is leaving us, and most importantly, leaving Taylor. It's important that she never feels alone in this world!

Suddenly this bullshit about Javier seemed…petty. Enough. This is me. Drama Queen. Sister. Friend. Daughter.

Hustler. And a bit of a temptress. Yup, they're all me, and I'm comfortable with it. I will love someone again, someone who doesn't disappear, who's as comfortable in his skin as Javier, but not as fucked up. I'll find him. But at that moment I just missed Javier.

Taylor was being her strong, resilient self, thinking about everybody else. "Hey," she said. Why don't you call Daniella—she's Javier's sister, right? She's in town with the show. Maybe she can give you some insight."

"Not a bad idea," I said.

When I called that afternoon, Daniella answered on the third ring and we caught up. She sounded soooo tired, and I knew she'd been working hard, but she managed to get me laughing about crazy things the dancers in *Romancing Vegas* were doing. "So...Ariana, what's up? I feel like you wanna ask me something."

Talking fast about Javier's sudden vanishing act, and trying to hold the tears back, I ended with "I know he's your brother, but why would he suddenly poof on me like that?"

"Poof? Oh, so suddenly you're not hearing from him? My brother does that to everyone." I could sense her mind working on what to advise, like I would if someone was grilling me about Anne. "Let me ask you," she said, "Is he going to Mexico to buy cars?"

"Yeah."

"That's it, then. He's focusing on the deals he has to make to keep himself profitable and keep the guys in the shop working. He's spinning the plates right now, lining up buyers, and keeping them excited about these cars. His business gets kind of intense in that phase."

"So he suddenly doesn't have time to see me, even to text me? If that's normal for him, I don't know. I don't want to be the bitchy girlfriend, but..."

"Ariana, I'm sorry, he's in the hunt right now. And if he likes you a lot, he's using this time to think about that. To him, that's normal." Daniella spoke extra clearly, as if I was a toddler having trouble following the logic. "Don't you get that?" She paused, choosing her words again. "You hardly lived with Jack and Cole, right? They're so much older than you guys. And your father, he wasn't around either? Have you ever lived with men?"

Huh, good point. "I guess, now that you mention it…not really. Just in the dorms freshman year."

"All right, then, here's the thing. Men don't juggle things like we do. They don't multitask, they focus. From what I can see, that's how men are, even your brother Jack. Not all men, but a lot of them. My dad was like that growing up, and Javier has always been that way. When they have a goal, other things just…fall by the wayside. Like you."

I could see what she was saying, but… "Well, not everything apparently. He told me he was leaving for Mexico. I had a meeting at the Flynn Bar, and he was there. He didn't notice me because he was having dinner with a hot brunette."

"Mierda!" Daniella hissed, "You got me on that one. Uuuuuhhhh. Don't know what to advise you. If it was Jack, I'd spring it on him in person when he wasn't expecting it. He's not a very good liar."

"Sounds like a plan. Meanwhile I hate my life."

"Don't do that. You are great for him, and I think one of the things he likes about you is that you don't give a shit, you're independent. Go semi-dark on him. Send him the three-word texts he's sending you. When he comes back and calls you, be very busy, you know what I mean? See what happens."

Chapter Twenty-One

Javier

M Y FIRST INSTINCT when I saw my mom was calling was not to answer. Yes, I was in Mexico, and yes, she lives in Mexico, but she lives four hours away, and I'm working. I don't have time to dick around and visit.

I was pretty glad I answered, though, because it appeared I'd fucked it up royally with Ariana. Our cell service kept dropping, so I could only understand about every third word, just enough to know Mom and Daniella wanted to kick my ass.

See, this is why I don't do relationships, especially with my sister's boyfriend's sister. Too much maintenance is involved when your sister and your mother decide they care about someone you're seeing. That's how you get an earful of "You haven't called, you haven't texted, she saw you when you were out to dinner at the Flynn with some brunette! Who the hell was that anyway, please tell me she's a client, and you're not a manwhore like your father?!"

And of course all of this was in very dirty, very angry Spanish. Since most of this info was transmitted via text (why do women like texting so much?), it was costing me about two bucks a word on my horrible international calling plan to find out I'm an idiot and a fuckboy.

Things are even worse when *you* care about the person you're seeing. Then you can't stop thinking about her and remembering the last time you had sex, how she looked when she came, what she said, what you said, and when is the next time you'll have sex. Oh, and you also fucking *miss* this person, and hate the idea that your bullshit caused the person you care about to be upset and in pain.

I tried calling Arianna, and I could kiiiinda hear a blurry version of her voice, just enough to know she couldn't hear me either. Same thing with voice mail, she texted (of course), saying:

Couldn't understand what u said, caught 'mom' and 'Daniella', guess u know.

After about 11 pm, when Mexicans finally stop doing business, I texted back:

U r upset cause I poofed. What I did before I left:

Research cars avail right now

Research buyers, call 2 check price expect

Check current DOT, EPA emission/safety rules, cost of fix

Check my Independent Commercial Importer status w DOT & EPA

Check if car is previous owned/registered USA (duty free), affects price offer

Deposit 2.5% taxes of total expected sale

Temporary license plates all cars "register import"

Flynn brunette, neighbor/dog care, works @ Flynn

Since here:

Check & negotiate 14 cars

Drive 700 miles doing above

This text cost $200, worth it
She texted back:
Sorry. Get it. Next time text 'Heart U, so busy'? Brunette touched u
I answered:
Can text heart u, can't help people touch, C you Thurs?
I laughed at her final:
Yes Thursday, I dog sit next time, graduation Friday

When I walked in my door Thursday afternoon, I was sure I was dead tired. Shuffling to the chair to take off my shoes, I looked around for the dogs and wandered into the living room. The dogs were lined up, contentedly napping on the couch and Ariana was at the head of the class, wearing sexy pink pumps, a polka dot apron, and nothing else. When I rushed to hold her, I said "These things, staying in touch and such, just don't occur to me when I'm…"

I never finished that sentence because Ariana threw her arms around my neck, her breasts pressing against my chest, her hips grinding into me until I thought I'd lose my mind. "I didn't want to appear too eager, this is me playing it cool."

She jumped up and wrapped her legs around my waist, moaning into my mouth, "Clothes, let's lose the clothes," unbuttoning my shirt and doing that licking thing on my piercing, followed by the nibble that sends an urgent command directly to my dick.

Waddling directly to my bedroom with her legs around me, I threw her on the bed. "Shouldn't I…shower first?" I choked out.

She giggled at the little bounce. "Next course, machote, after the hors d'oeuvres. Can't you see I was cooking?"

"Machote, tough guy, is it?" I slid down her body, licking,

kissing and sucking on her perfect tits and that little red landing strip pointing to her heavenly pussy. "Well, what if I'm not hungry right now, Belleza?"

She stared at me, I stared at her. I saw her chin lift as she took off her apron, challenging me. "The food is hot and ready, so I think you should eat now." I collapsed next to her on the bed, both of us laughing our asses off at the ridiculous banter. but laughing soon dissolved into…what *she* said.

The cares of the past week fell away while we got lost in each other with kisses and moans, grinding and pounding, whispering *harder, deeper* and *more*.

This isn't fucking, this is making love, I thought. I wanted to show her that, show her I love her. Those fancy thoughts went up in smoke when lightning shot up my spine, setting fire to my brain until I heard myself say, "Ariana, I love you Ariana!" The sound made me come just that much harder when I heard her say it back to me.

In the shower, Ariana scrubbed my back a little too hard. "You know it doesn't count to say 'I love you' when you come, right?"

"I did hear that somewhere," I said, massaging the shampoo into her scalp the way she likes it. "When *does* it count?"

"Mmmmm, you'll feel it when it's right."

"Okay, so we're a couple of people who didn't want to commit, talking about love. Funny, right? Are we both still wondering who's going to be out the door first?"

"I'll flip you for it," she said. I didn't like that answer, so I dumped the entire contents of a plastic bucket of water on her. She wiped her eyes and put her arms around me. "But meanwhile, I'd like to be with you."

"Just me? Are we talking exclusive and moving in together here?"

"I am. Can you handle that?"

"Sure. I can, actually." The whole conversation was oddly comfortable, like the perfect business negotiation. Maybe not right for others, but perfect for Ariana and me.

Chapter Twenty-Two

Ariana

ANNE WAS WAITING for me at a corner table at our coffee shop, and she'd already ordered two of our absolute favorite, ultimate coffee drinks—Italian Affogato, espresso with vanilla ice cream and cookies. The last time she did this, she pitched me on the idea of upgrading our lame-ass website and getting a warehouse and a part-time person to run Two Much because she felt overwhelmed.

Of course, it involved giving up the profits we'd been saving for an apartment and spending on two-hundred-dollar UGGs and running shoes. I mean, a girl has to reward herself, right? Wrong. Something tells me Anne and Warren Buffett, the frugal billionaire King of Investors who drives an old car, could easily be besties.

So the news that day was that Anne wants to pursue a teaching certificate and master's degree to work with kids with disabilities in middle and high school. She slid a brochure from an online degree program across the table, something about "...helping students with successful transitions from school to independent living."

Leaning toward me, she said "I don't know what it is, but

the minute I started looking at it, I knew it was want I want to do, you know? I thought about studying teaching back in high school, but..." Her explanation seemed a little stiff and rehearsed, as if she was uncertain how I'd feel about the whole thing. "I'm sorry Ariana, I..."

"Why would you feel you have to apologize for wanting to do that? I'm happy for you! Go for it. And, by the way, I saw the video of Laura's speech at her graduation. Fantastic! I could tell you fixed her hair, she looked so cute."

"I knooooow! Laura's speech has become a viral video hit. I sent the video to our friends, who sent it to their friends and...well, you know how that goes. Now the SNU people asked if she would give the speech at our graduation!" We both laughed and she covered my hand with hers. "As far as the teaching thing, well, I kind of ended up following you into the business major, and we talked about growing the Two Much website together, but..."

"The not-together part, that's what's bothering you about this. So...it's an online course, you're still living here in Las Vegas, right? Hopefully with a tall, hottie warehouse manager?"

She nodded, her eyes a little teary.

I got up from my chair and sat next to her on the bench, giving her an affectionate squeeze and a noogie. "We've always done everything together, but...we're kind of officially grown up now, don't you think?"

"Yeah, but...Jack and Cole are twins, and they still work together, even though they're pushing forty!"

"It's not a rule, though, just an unusual example. And they're not as cool as we are."

She laughed, but crinkled her nose, searching for the right words. "So does this mean I'm officially un-twinning you?" Her breath hitched. "I don't want to un-twin you Rainbow Brite!"

"You could never un-twin me, no matter how hard you try!" I squeezed her again. "Speaking of this, though, here's what I'm thinking about our possible future living arrangements. I hear we might soon be enjoying a rooftop pool together and some other very attractive, uh, lifestyle enhancements. Of course, we'd have to chip in on the condo payments so we don't feel like freeloaders, but somehow I think the handsome owners will offer us a very good deal, don't you?"

When I winked, Anne agreed and said, "You're right, we can't un-twin each other! And somehow, miraculously, Owen and Javier seem okay with that."

Chapter Twenty-Three

Anne

"WHOSE IDEA WAS it to wear high heels today?" I gave Ariana the pointy eye while we walked across campus in our caps and gowns and bare feet, carrying our stupid shoes. Parking for graduation was about a mile from where we had to be, so we were hobbling over there, carefully avoiding stones and broken glass. We took our assigned seats and put our shoes on, crossing the stage to pick up our diplomas with heads held high. Feeling about as special as you can feel when you're graduating with two thousand other students (and that was only half the class, A through H), we looked forward to seeing everybody after the speeches.

The commencement speakers talked about the usual stuff, you know, go for your dreams, live life with integrity, learn from the universe, seize the day. But Owen's sister Laura had everyone on the edge of their seats, wondering what this young woman was going to say. She started out by talking about how it was great sometimes to fly under the radar. "Well, for me that's automatic," she said. "People see I'm Downs, and they don't expect much. For some people high expectations work, but I like it when they're pleasantly surprised. It's like when you look at a kiwi or an avocado. They're kind of ugly from the outside but when you peel the ugly off, you're amazed at how wonderful it is. Don't you wonder about the first person who saw a chicken poop out an egg and said 'I'll bet that will taste delicious, I can't wait to try it!'"

Everyone laughed at that, and I imagined how proud Owen must be, watching her up there. And I was proud of him for helping make this day possible for her. What sixteen-year-old guy does something like that? I read somewhere that 'Saints are sinners who kept trying,' and I guess that's what he did.

Laura's speech was about hanging around with the right people. "Surround yourself with people who inspire you and make you feel happy to be you. Not one of you is here today because you did it by yourself, so keep doing that for the rest of your life." I thought about the idea that finding the right person, Owen, didn't make me totally focus on the relationship. Instead it freed me up to new strengths I didn't know I had. Other people must've felt the same way, because the applause was deafening.

Of all the people we could talk to right after, who'd have guessed it would be Sanjay and his fiancée?

Sanjay introduced us, and she was wonderful, talking to everyone so graciously. When she walked away, Sanjay said to us "We grew up together, and our parents are in the same business. She's so great, smart. Our parents are powerful people, but when they arranged the marriage with her, I felt like I was being told what to do. I'm sorry you got caught in the middle of my rebellion, Ariana, truly sorry. I had to realize the problem, and now I want to marry her. But I'm sorry, you deserved better."

Ariana agreed. "Yes, I do deserve better. And who knows?

I looked at your fiancée, her intelligence and humor, and wondered if maybe she rebelled and has her secrets too. I hope so."

Touché, my sista! I thought, hugging her for the hundredth time.

When Javier and Ariana talked to Mom and Taylor, Javier held my sister's hand and said, "You know I love your daughter don't you?" Mom's eyes welled up, and she gave him a big hug.

"Your dad and Mario are meeting us at the restaurant for lunch," she said to me. *Holy shit! Only Mom would have the boyfriend wait for us with the husband she never bothered to divorce!*

We were all thinking about Taylor's mom, about the fact that she wasn't here. We knew it would take a helluva lot of high water to keep Tina away from our graduation. "She's bad, isn't she?" I asked. Her lips trembling, Taylor nodded, wiping tears from her cheeks.

I knew Mom liked Owen, first because he's great, but also because... did I mention he has red hair? He wears it very short, but it is unmistakably red. Ariana's and my red hair is from Mom's side, and when two people with red hair have a kid, that kid will be a redhead. She was thinking about that when she checked him out, I just know it!

"It's so nice to see you again," she said to him. They walked toward the parking lot, talking and laughing, having such a great time, it was almost annoying!

It hadn't occurred to me before that Owen might need some mothering like everyone else. Good times, very good times ahead!

Don't you think Anne and Ariana's friend Taylor Spiros is due for some good times?! I do too!

Read an excerpt from Taylor's story as it will appear in the 2017 novel.

Excerpt from

Eight Days
of
Yes

KARA KEEN

Prologue

HAVE YOU EVER hit SEND and then immediately wished you hadn't? I swear, when I've had a few drinks, some other woman possesses me and makes me uninhibited to the point of stupidity. I mean, I *like* myself when I'm tipsy Taylor, but still. Actions *do* have consequences.

The bright light coming in the bedroom window is not my friend, but the curtain is open because I face-planted onto the bed with all my clothes on after a fun evening of drinking with my besties. I have a headache, a dry mouth, an upset stomach and a bad, bad, BAD case of drinker's remorse. Or maybe it's messaging remorse, similar to texting remorse, 'cause I'm okay with the actual drinking. Honestly, after everything I've been through lately, I needed to get out of my own head for a few hours. What I DO feel stupid about is Facebook messaging someone I barely know last night while I was drunk enough to think going on a free cruise with a stranger was a great idea.

Going through the stages of Sender's Denial, I open my eyes and think *No, you didn't, oh no you didn't, OHNOYOUDIN'T!!!* When I drag my phone off the nightstand, of course I open up Messenger for the fourth...no the fifth time. And there it is, a post from a random woman named Reina who used to belong to our soccer league ranting about her really nice brother.

And there's my reply, with my slightly drunken photo and my phone number! My phone number, people! There's no do-overs in Facebookland when you private-message someone. What's done is...you did it! You think you can take stuff down, but it's always there, archived somewhere by someone. Hoping that maybe it changed while I wasn't looking directly at it, I tap the post and read it for the bajillionth time:

Ladies - would you like to go on a free eight-day cruise around Hawaii? This is legit! Let me say first, my brother may kill me for putting this out here like this but I just have to! He was planning to propose to his girlfriend (who I knew was bad news from the start) on this cruise, but she broke up with him and it's too late to get a refund. The cruise is from May 10 through the 18th, with a day on either end for your flights in and out. If you're under 30 and single or you have a great single friend you want to tag on this, reply by Friday if you're interested with a pic and phone number (he's not a texting or messenging type guy). I'll see him on Saturday and talk him into calling one of you and getting together. I attached his pic, and my goal is to convince you he's a great guy if I do say so myself! This is not a hookup, just a chance for both of you to have a great time.

Chapter One

Taylor Spiros

9 p.m. the night before

66 "TAYLOR, I THINK you need to bust out of this... funk you're in. Do something totally crazy!" Of course my friend Ariana would say that, she does crazy things all the time and gets away with it. I pretended not to understand, though.

"Bust out of what?" I took a sip of my drink, pulling out the yellow stick with the fruit on it and eating a chunk of pineapple.

Anne took the tiny umbrella from the drink and stuck it in the beaded hairband I was wearing. "Theeerrre you go," she giggled, tipsy after one drink. "Now you look ready for an exotic adventure!" Anne is Ariana's identical twin sister, and the two of them are a force of nature who could convince the Pope he wasn't Catholic.

Ariana took both my hands in hers, and lowered her voice, speaking in the patient tone of a nursery school teacher. "You have been through years of hell, worrying your mom's breast cancer would come back. Then it fucking did come back, and she was so sick. God, you took such good care of her! Then you got punched in the gut when she died. You've been walking around in a daze for five months, going through Mama Tina's stuff and selling the house." My mom Tina used to babysit Anne, Ariana and me when we were little; thus, 'Mama Tina', Mom to us all.

I tried to pull my hands away, shaking my head. "You say all this like I don't know, or like there's actually something I can do about the way I feel." In my mind, it was more like *It's actually more a problem of what I* don't *feel which is...* anything. *I felt numb.* "I don't have a job, and there's a big-ass gap on my resume. The financial stuff from Mom's estate isn't done yet, so I can't buy a condo. I'm couch-surfing at your place and your mom's house. What do you want me to do, get a puppy?"

Anne thought that was hilarious. "Suuuure! Just house train it before you bring it to our place." See, that "our place" was another thing. Both my friends were suddenly coupled up, living in condos in the same building with their boyfriends, Owen and Javier. Wonderful, amazing boyfriends. And I'm...not.

"I'm thinking we need to set you up an internet dating profile." Ariana lifted her chin, oozing determination and focus. When she's like that, resistance is futile. Her plan is a done deal.

I groaned. "By 'we,' I gather you mean me? Isn't that just for the desperate and the crazies?"

"Oh, my God, Taylor, where have you been? Under a rock?! Everyone uses dating sites now." I could see Ariana was in full mastermind mode now, drumming her fingers on the table. "Yeah, but...are we talking Match or Tinder? Are we shopping for love or some casual hookups?"

"Seriously? There are legit hookup sites now? The guys

don't even have to *pretend* they're looking for a relationship anymore?" I took an extra-long slug of my drink, freaked just thinking about it.

Anne whipped out her phone and showed me a site where your whole profile is eight photos and 1200 characters. "As you can see," she said, "this app is all about the photos, about what you look like. If you like the person you swipe right, if not, swipe left. Then anyone who's right-swiped can start messaging you and you can make plans to meet. Or not. They say you have to kiss seventy-five frogs before you find your prince, and this, uh, I guess, helps speed up the process. A lot."

Of course, Ariana had personally experienced this app. "Ohhhh, when it first came out, I was obsessed, I went on seven dates in two weeks. They were all asswipes. Then I quit." Ariana showed me a handsome guy's profile on her phone and sighed. "People lie a lot. If it's a shirtless photo in the mirror, that's a definite no. But still, you could meet him somewhere and be like, 'Uhhh...you don't look like your pictures.' And he'll count on the fact that you'll be polite and get to know him anyway. Luckily, I met Javier without this, and I don't have to go back on it again, 'cause I probably would have. It's addicting. You find yourself thinking that Prince Charming is always right around the corner."

"I'm sorry, this all seems so...brutal. I don't think I could handle it emotionally right now." Tilting my head back, I downed the rest of my drink. "And, P.S., I have kind of been under a rock when you think about it. My recent boyfriends had one thing in common—they worked in either a hospital or rehab. I met them while taking care of Mom."

We were all quiet for a minute and I nodded when the bartender offered to get me another drink. My eyes filled up with tears, thinking about Mom being so sick but charming various guys into asking me out. How could she just…not *be* here? I keep expecting to walk into the living room and find her lying there in her rented hospital bed, reading a book. Now someone else owns the living room. Maybe that's a good thing. Since I sold the house, I only think of her every ten minutes instead of every five.

I stuck the umbrella from my new drink in my hair, next to the other one. "I told you the story about the most recent one, right, the doctor? Mom fixed me up with him."

"Oh right, the doctor who turned out to be addicted to amphetamines." Ariana didn't look at me when she said that; she was busy typing something on her phone.

"Yeah," I sighed, "that one. Too bad. He was really cute. We were on our third date when the police came to pick him up."

"You said that," Anne said, slurring her words a little. "So…third date. Were you planning on…uh, you know. Were you going to sleep with him? After observing the three-date rule?"

"God, listen to you, sis!" Ariana chuckled. "You used to avoid talking about sex, and now you're, like, obsessed with it."

"Yeah, now that you're gettin' some, you know the rules, huh, Anne?" I said. "You and Owen followed the work-together-for-a-year-and-a-half rule before you even sat on his lap, and then decided to have sex, is that what I'm hearing?"

We all laughed, Anne blushing scarlet.

"And yes, I was kinda hoping Doctor Speedy liked me that way. He was a good kisser, and he did this thing where he walked me out to my Uber and opened the door for me, kind of adorable." I sighed again. "Do you think I should try for a conjugal visit while he's in jail?"

We laughed so hard at that one, the 35-ish guy sitting at

the bar next to Ariana offered to buy us a round. We accepted. "I couldn't help hearing what you ladies were talking about," he said after introductions. His name was Victor. "I met my wife on Craigslist. That was ten years ago. Do people still use that?"

"Yeah," I chimed in. "My roommate used that a couple times in college. Met some douchebags, but a few nice guys, too." I stuck the third paper umbrella in my hair, feeling quite a nice buzz at that point. This evening was honestly the most fun I'd had in such a long, long time.

Still typing on her phone, Ariana said, "Sorry, people, Craigslist can be a vast wasteland of desperate men writing 'suck my cock' in all caps and including a photo of the aforementioned body part."

Victor's eyes widened at Ariana's casual use of that phrase, but he countered, "I've heard people meet people on Facebook now, like the friend of your friend's friend might be the one."

"Apparently many people are confused about exactly what The One means these days." Ariana grinned. "And by people, I mean dudes. But…yeah, I actually do know someone who recently met someone on Facebook. And it's free. Is that good or bad?'"

"Well," our new friend gave a little bow, leaving a tip on the bar, "I don't know if it's good and I'm glad I'm married. I apologize for my entire gender." Looking at me he added, "Happy hunting to you, and all the best."

"Okay, here's the plan," Ariana announced as he walked away. "Tomorrow we meet at my salon and we get Taylor's hair cut and blown out, along with professional makeup. I'll bring some wardrobe choices for our photo shoot, and we'll come up with some nice shots to put on Match. I've already written your profile and set up a fake email address. Anne and I will preview the avalanche of emails you're going to be getting, and show you only the good ones. You're right, you don't need a bunch of sleazoids propositioning you right now."

"Uh…okay…I guess? Won't we be lying if my hair looks all straight, not my usual Greek-girl curly hair?" My last name is Spiros, and I have the curly hair to prove it.

Stepping back and assessing, Anne framed me up like a photographer. "She's right. I think we should do kind of a Greek goddess thing, half up and half down. Let the curls do their thing, they're beautiful."

"Spoken like a true, straight-haired white girl named Carleton," I snorted.

Ariana crossed her arms, unhappy but outvoted. "Fine," she said, pursing her lips. "Greek goddess it is. And I recently read that more natural photos get a better response, you seem more…uh…trustworthy."

I took out my phone and shot a selfie, raising my arm high so my cleavage and the paper umbrellas in my hair were prominent in the photo. Ariana looked at it and laughed. "That's a little *too* natural!"

Checking it on my screen, I liked the mischief in my eyes and the slight drunkety-drunk smile on my lips, which is weird 'cause I always hate pics of myself. I probably like it *'cause* I'm drunkety drunk, right? I crowded my girls, my identical bookend dearest friends, against my shoulders and took a pic of the three of us. "Okay ladies, our plans are set for tomorrow, then! So cool that we can walk to your place from here, our favorite bar." Outside, we hooked arms together, taking up the whole sidewalk, and skipped down the street singing "We're off to see the Wizaaaaard!"

Ariana's boyfriend Javier lives in a brand new condo on the ground floor of the old warehouse building three blocks away, and his four dogs started barking like maniacs when Ariana keyed into the place. I was sooo in the mood for some doggy lovin', and threw myself on the couch so John, Paul, George and Ringo could lick my face and I could scratch their ears and warm, soft bellies. They were a motley crew of medium-sized shelter mutts with varying amounts of pug, boxer and pit bull in their ancestry. I realized I'd been living kind of a solitary existence there for a while, going through all the stuff in our family home after my mother died. I missed being touched, the casual hugs and pecks on the cheek of family living, and these cuddly dogs were filling a void I hadn't realized was there.

"We just missed Javier," Ariana said, reading her phone as always. "He's meeting someone at the Flynn Hotel, the Umbrella Bar."

"Who's he meeting," Anne asked, "his grandmother?" That particular bar was lovely, but tended toward an older crowd.

"No," Ariana smiled, plopping herself next to me and pulling Ringo onto her lap. "But close. He's meeting his accountant, Michael." I pictured a silver-haired man in a three-piece suit. As usual, Ariana read my mind. "Michael is actually Javier's age, late 20's, but he's... a little, uh, *stiff* you might say. I'd introduce you, but I hear he's getting engaged."

I laughed and pulled her hair. "Don't do me any favors, girlfriend! I don't need a guy like that, I need a bad boy, a sexy guy like Javier, a free spirit! Know any more of those?"

She and Anne laughed, elbowing me in the ribs and piling dogs on my lap. "Rrrriiiiight, a sexy bad boy for Taylor, we'll order that right up!" Apparently, I have a good-girl image earned by taking care of my mother for years and years. *That* girl might actually *not* know what to do with a guy like Javier.

I exhaled my third big sigh of the evening. "Okay, I know, I know, no bad boys for Taylor! But it's fun to think about, right?" We sat on the couch watching an episode of *Sex and the City* for the umpty-umpth time, and soon both my girls were snoozing, the dogs curled up on their bellies. I swear, dogs are so much better than a sleeping pill!

Thinking about what Ariana said about Facebook, I got on my laptop and was immediately sucked in. I haven't been that active on Facebook because, let's face it—there aren't a lot of Facebook moments when you're taking care of a cancer patient. I scrolled through my notifications and a few friends liked a post from a few days ago by someone named Reina Ross who apparently used to play in the Sin City Coed Soccer League that Anne and Ariana organized. Ariana tagged me and sent me a little winky face as her comment. Knowing Ariana, I'm sure she didn't actually read what Reina's post was about but probably thought the guy in the picture was kind of cute.

And he was attractive in a generic kind of way, looking fit but kind of like every guy with short hair you've ever seen working in a bank. Wearing jeans and a "Bacon makes everything better" T-shirt, he was sitting on a rock, apparently trying to look ruggedly sporty. Instead he appeared uncomfortable, as if the rock was poking him in the butt. It was the kind of picture a sister would take, saying "C'mon bro, just relax!" He had a nice smile, though. Reina, the sister of the guy in the pic, was obviously trying to help the guy out with his crazy problem, acting as kind of a character witness to the single ladies who might reply to this post:

Ladies - would you like to go on a free eight-day cruise around Hawaii? This is legit! Let me say first, my brother may kill me for putting this out here like this but I just have to! He was planning to propose to his girlfriend (who I knew was bad news from the start) on this cruise, but she broke up with him and it's too late to get a refund. The cruise is from May 10 through the 18th, with a day on either end for your flights in and out. If you're under 30 and single... and etcetera. In my buzzy state of mind, Reina's proposition seemed like an interesting and viable thing to do.

Hmmm. Bust out, do something totally crazy... I found myself hitting reply and typing a message.

Hey Reina, I'm between jobs right now, and I'm available to go on that cruise! You may remember me from the soccer league, I'm Anne and Ariana's friend and teammate. I'm 24 years old, a college graduate, and I live in the Las Vegas area, and I'm assuming your brother does as well, since you mentioned flying out of here. I'm sorry about your brother's breakup, but hope we can meet in person soon to see if...to discuss...to explore... I kept stumbling over that last line, typing, backspacing and retyping.

What exactly would we talk about if we got together? I guess the usual first date nonsense—what was your major, what do you do for work, your favorite social media, movie, music, book, television show. I am so out of touch with dating chit-chat, having become more proficient at discussing the side effects of different kinds of sedatives and chemotherapy than who killed who on *Game of Thrones*? (Isn't someone always killing someone on that show?) Anyway, I finally came up with a last line that I thought was hopeful and upbeat.

I'm sorry about your brother's breakup, but hope we can meet in person soon to plan our wonderful adventure.

Salesmen call that "the assumed close," where you move beyond the initial question by assuming they're taking the deal. (My degree is in marketing, in case you were wondering.) I added my phone number and attached the picture with the three umbrellas in my hair after realizing it was the only recent photo I had. And then I pressed Send.

You would think I would be panicking about some stranger who could be a weirdo having a picture of me and my phone number. But no, I wasn't panicking about *that*. I walked over to the tall windows and looked out at Javier's very pleasant yard, freaking about the fact that I wrote that I was "between jobs." Pressing my hands against the glass, I imagined talking to the guy in the picture, sitting in a coffee shop wearing an outfit I agonized over for days—*too dressy? Too casual? Trying too hard?* Everything is going well until he asks me, "So you said you were between jobs. What were you doing, and why did you leave?"

A giant lump swelled in my throat when I thought about my reply. What should I say? "My full time job for the past two years was taking care of my mother. She had cancer. I failed at my job, and she died." I hadn't cried very often since the funeral, but I was making up for it then.

In *Two Much* you met Daniella, the amazing dancer who stars in the show *Romancing Vegas*!

Turn the page and read this excerpt about Daniella and Jack. Then get the whole story in Kara Keen's novel *Romancing Vegas*, available now in all formats wherever books are sold!

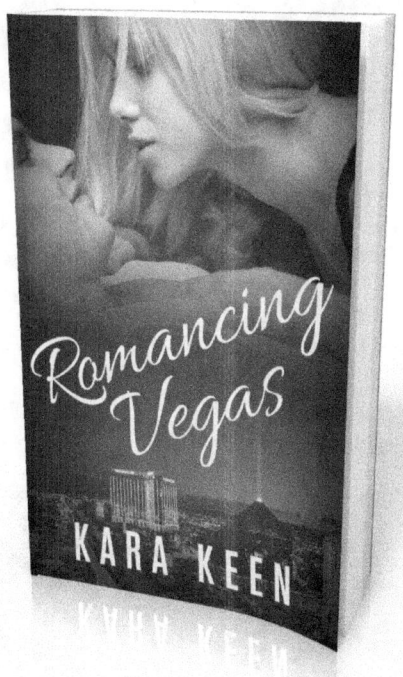

Daniella didn't plan to fall for Anne and Ariana's brother Jack, but she couldn't stop thinking about the crazy, sexy times they shared.

Jack is into fast, edgy living and so much fun—but is he ready to ditch the Peter Pan act and be her Number One?

Chapter Ten

DANIELLA DECIDED TO wear a dress for Thanksgiving, celebrating this opportunity to see her mother again. She felt good about it, admiring the pies she baked for dinner, until Jack came to pick her up, roaring up to her apartment on his motorcycle. Okay, he looked hot, his tall, muscular body in a pair of well-worn jeans and a fitted black T-shirt, but seriously...

"Are you fucking kidding me? You want my dad to see you bring me on a motorcycle? You are such a big kid." That stung, especially 'cause they both knew she was right.

"You mean an old kid?"

"No, a big, overgrown Peter Pan kid! We have to rent a car, Jack. They live all the way in Boulder City."

"On Thanksgiving? Uh...let me make a few calls." He left and came back about an hour later in a bright yellow Porsche 911.

"Really Jack? You rented a Porsche?"

"The other choice was this thing." He showed her a pic on his phone. *Oh. Okay.* Even she couldn't deny that the green troll car had been hit by an ugly stick.

Looking over at him, she noticed he'd shaved and put on a collared shirt and dress slacks. "Jack, I'm sorry I'm being such a bitch. Thank you for renting the car and...uh...you look so nice. Thank you. I'm just nervous to see my mom and all."

When they pulled up to a sprawling ranch house, Daniella's brother came out to greet them, a tall, powerful-looking man in his late 20's, with shaggy black hair and dark eyes.

"Jack, this is Javier," said Daniella. "We're very proud of him. He started his own company, import/export, and he's doing very well."

"Not as well as you, apparently," Javier said to Jack, gazing at the yellow Porsche as if it were a gorgeous blonde.

"Oh, it's rented," said Jack. "My brother and I share a car, and he got there first. Would you like to drive this?"

Javier couldn't jump in the driver's seat fast enough. "Let's go." Daniella went inside with the pies.

Jack jumped in and the tires squealed when Javier pulled away in a hurry, making the Porsche purr through its paces. "Have you driven one of these before?" Jack asked. "You're good."

"I've taken a couple of test drives. Just dream building," he answered, hitting a long stretch of highway and letting the car loose. "So you're a cruise ship captain, wow." He didn't look away from the road, "I saw one in Long Beach harbor, and that sucker was huge. Is it hard to drive that thing around?"

"We use computers a lot, but yeah, my brother and I have sixteen years and lots of licenses for piloting ships. It takes experience."

Javier still kept his eyes forward. "Speaking of that, aren't you a little old for my sister?"

Jack laughed and slapped his thigh. "Dude, you don't beat around the bush, do you? But to answer your question, there's a big age difference, but for some reason she puts up with me."

He figured it was time to change the subject. "Let me show you how to put this car in insane mode. You tap this screen and go from 416 horsepower to 691!" In a fraction of a second, the car leapt forward and Jack's head slammed back against the seat.

"Goooooddamn!" Javier hollered. "This baby has an awesomely low center of gravity. Wooooo-Hoo!"

"Wow, your brother is kind of...intense," Jack whispered to Daniella when they got back.

"Ya' think? Yeah, he's like my dad that way. They like to be in control." She had an apron on, and he thought it was adorable. "Can you believe it? Javier remembered to put the turkey in, but nothing else has even been started. Men."

He shook hands with Santiago, her father, and tried to strike up a conversation, but after a few minutes the man walked away to watch the game. Jack pulled an apron on. "Hey, not all men suck in the kitchen. Tell me what to do, and we'll get this show on the road."

He got a kick out of her freestyle save on the cooking, and they got everything going in short order. Her teenage sister Sofia pitched in too, smiling shyly at Jack when he kissed her cheek and said, "We're a good team, aren't we?" Soon the kitchen smelled delicious.

Daniella smiled, hugging him. "I thought with four sisters you'd be spoiled, but I guess your mom made you toe the line. Good for her! I like a well-trained man." She walked into the den where her father and brother were watching TV. "Aren't one of you guys picking Mom up at the airport?"

"She wanted to take a cab," Javier replied.

"You know your mom, she has her ways," grumbled her father.

When dinner was almost ready, the doorbell rang, and Daniella opened it. "Uh...Hi, Mom." Jack walked over to see why Daniella sounded weird and saw a pretty woman come in holding a tiny baby, Daniella trailing behind with a bunch of baby stuff. "Jack this is my mom Regina, and this is..."

"Mateo, he's six weeks old. Nice to meet you Jack." She settled the sleeping baby into his infant seat and threw her arms around Daniella and Sofia. "Oh, I've missed you girls soooo much!"

Santiago didn't seem to be in any hurry to greet his wife, glaring at her with his hands on his hips. Javier came over and hugged her, gesturing at the baby. "So what's the story with the baby, Mom?" Javier was actually her stepson, Santiago's son from his first marriage, but she'd raised him as her own for twenty of his twenty-seven years.

She drew herself up tall. "This is my son Mateo, named after his father, the man I've been living with in Mexico." All breathing in the room stopped, and everyone stared silently from the baby to his mother and back.

Santiago screamed at his wife, *"Maldita puta! Me averguenzas delante de nuestros hijos!"* and stormed out of the house, the door slamming behind him with a bang.

Jack put his hand on Daniella's shoulder to comfort her. "Are you wondering what he said?" Daniella's mother asked, looking at Jack. "He said, 'Fucking whore! You embarrassed me in front of my children!'"

Javier was standing in front of the window, wringing his hands as he watched his father peel out of the driveway. "What is this!? A fucking telenovela?!"

Daniella and her mom exchanged glances and started cackling, working their way up to full-on roaring with laughter and holding each other for support, they were laughing so hard. They'd watched the novela *Morellia* together for years, it was their thing, and this situation was right out of the show's typical script.

When Jack asked, "What's a telenovela?" that was it, they completely lost it, tears running down their cheeks as they collapsed on the couch, pulling poor, confused teenage Sofia into their laps and stroking her hair.

"It's a soap opera in Spanish," said Daniella, gasping for breath and wiping tears from her cheeks. Sniffing the air, she bolted off the couch and said, "Oh, shit! The turkey's burning!" and disappeared into the kitchen.

She came out in a few minutes. "It's ooookay, the bird is ready, and so is everything else. Let's talk while we eat, since Mateo's still sleeping."

Everyone helped get the food on the table, and Javier did his best to carve the turkey, cursing his father for leaving him with the unfamiliar task. He remained surly, stabbing his food and shifting in his chair. Jack could picture Cole reacting the exact same way, pissed at the world for something no one could control. Daniella seemed resilient, handling whatever came her way, kind of an old soul. He was really impressed with her.

Regina ate quickly, nursed Mateo, and sat back down at the table with them. Daniella enjoyed holding the baby, kissing his sweet face and cooing at him.

Regina leaned forward, her expression intent. "Sofia, some of this may be hard to hear, but you're old enough to hear it now." Her glance took them all in. "Your father has no right to be angry about this. He cheated on me all the time. The man I'm with now, Mateo's father, is faithful and kind, and I love him. I've asked Santiago for a divorce. He knew about everything before I arrived today, and I hope you'll urge him to get that rolling so I can marry Mateo's father."

She sagged into her chair, shoulders drooping, and let out a long sigh. "Javier and Daniella, I know you guys have work here and..." she looked at Jack, "...other commitments, but I'm going to be living in Mexico. I'll stay here a while, but I hope you'll come and stay with us, Sofia, either full or part time...whatever you want to do. You're an American citizen, so there's no worries about that, sweetheart."

Kissing the top of Sofia's head, she choked out "You don't have to decide right now, but I hope you'll think about it seriously." She and Sofia embraced, rocking back and forth and crying, and Daniella handed the baby to her brother to hold while she and Jack started clearing the table.

They cleaned up the kitchen together in silence until Regina came in a while later with Mateo and a collapsible stroller. "Daniella, I'd like us to go for a walk together. I have something I need to tell you. You can invite Jack or not, it's your choice." She seemed pleased when Daniella tugged at Jack's hand and they all walked outside. It was a lovely 70 degrees and sunny, Jack's favorite time of year in Vegas.

Holding hands with Daniella, Regina let Jack push the stroller. "Soooo...it seems to be a day of revelations," Regina said, "and there's something I've been meaning to tell you, Daniella." She stopped and took both of Daniella's hands in hers. "I'm not your biological mother. You are the daughter of a woman Santiago had an affair with, also an illegal."

She raised an eyebrow. "I'm noticing a pattern here, aren't you? When your underage mother was deported right after you were born, she left you with us so you could be raised as an American."

Jack searched Daniella's face and saw nothing. She seemed numb, like she was having trouble processing everything.

Regina continued. "You are my daughter in every important way, and I love you so much. For me, this knowledge changes nothing, and I hope it's the same for you. I've been in touch with your mother in Mexico, and she'd love to meet you if that's ever your wish. If it's your choice to share this with Javier and Sofia you can, if not...it's up to you." She took Daniella in her arms, catching Jack's eye over her shoulder. "I'm glad this friend of yours is here to talk with you about it and drive you back to the city."

Daniella leaned back, her eyes glassy but her lips smiling. "I love you, Mom. I don't know what to think about the other stuff, but...I just love you so much. I'm glad you found someone and you're happy." Giving her mom a squeeze and grabbing the stroller from Jack, she started walking and added, "But this really *is* like the novelas, isn't it?" They all had another good laugh at that.

After eating Daniella's delicious pies for dessert, there were lots more hugs, and Regina promised to come watch Daniella rehearse. When they got in the car, Jack was thinking he was so glad he'd been there for her on this wacko day, and he didn't want her to be alone. "Will you come back to my place tonight, stay with me?" he asked.

"Sure, yes. We have to stop by my place and pick up my pills, though." She'd started on birth control pills a week ago. Massaging the back of his neck, she said, "You...surprised me today."

"How? In a good way or a bad way?

"Good, definitely good. I thought you'd be turned off, kind of hang back from all the craziness. But you were right in there, keeping everything kind of...normal. As normal as possible, I guess. Even kind of cheerful. I guess you have to deal with crazies on the ship, even crazier than my family."

He pressed into her hand, enjoying the massage. "Uh...yes, yes I do. And as far as dealing with things, uh...your Mom moved into the master bedroom with the baby. Where is your dad going to sleep when he comes back? Is there going to be trouble, is your mom safe? Where does he work…does he have somewhere else to go?"

"Oh, shit. Didn't think of that. Let me ask my mom." Jack was glad she called her Mom without hesitating. Regina had kept her American cell phone and picked up right away. They spoke in rapid Spanish.

"What'd she say?"

Daniella laughed. "I'm quoting here." Speaking in a perfect imitation of her mother's spicy accent, she said, "'Your father called Javier to tell him he'll be staying with his latest whore while I'm here. What did you think, he was waiting for me? Huh! I knew better.'"

The warm air felt amazing on her skin, her hair blowing around while the convertible sliced through the humid desert twilight. "How do people get to this point? What's it all about, Jack?"

"Fuck if I know." His shoulders were tight, his jaw clenched. "It was a hell of a crazy day, for sure."

She shifted in her seat, trying to get his attention, but he kept his eyes glued to the road. Daniella was ready to think about something else. "Is it about this?" she asked, her voice breathy.

"Wh…?" When he turned to look at her, she was sitting there with her top off, wearing nothing above the waist but an evil smile.

A grin pulling at his lips, he looked back at the road. "Yeah, it's definitely about that."

She hiked up her skirt, her lacy stockings and garter belt in full view. "So… is it about this too?"

His voice was a little tighter now. "You were wearing that…the whole day?"

"Yes."

He pulled off the road abruptly and parked behind a stand of mesquite and sugar pine. While she was looking for her shirt on the floor, Jack yanked open her car door. "Don't put that on."

"Uh...okay."

Continue the adventures of Jack and Daniella in
Romancing Vegas!

Kara Keen

TOP 10 AMAZON AUTHOR

After a career in public relations and advertising, Kara Keen got tired of writing half-truths and decided to write the whole truth—love is all you need! After writing the first three books in the *Captain's Orders* series of sizzling contemporary romance, she focuses on New Adult romance in *Two Much* and the upcoming *Eight Days of Yes.*

Placing her characters in exciting destinations, she enjoys guiding them through emotional situations and sophisticated adventures. More importantly, readers and reviewers of her novels appreciate how her characters heal each other through wise-cracking humor, honest talk, doing the right thing, and really hot sex!

Kara wrote two nonfiction books (under a different name) about sex, intimacy, and women's health, and spoke at conferences across the country. Recognizing that the brain is a woman's most important sex organ, she started writing stories to fire up women's minds about the many ways men and women get together. Hanging out with her family in northern Virginia, she has no problem sharing the secrets of writing—read a lot, connect with other writers and keep your butt in the chair until you reach your goal for the day! As writers and most professions will agree, it's not just a matter of inspiration but of perspiration (putting in the time and effort).

If you enjoyed *Two Much* and want to read about Anne and Ariana's big brothers, read *Captain's Orders* and *Romancing Vegas*! Yes, it does feature new characters—Primo and Oksana, Tania and Cole, Daniella and Jack. But they are totally different and unique stories you'll love. Also check out the story of Anne and Ariana's big sister Liz in the new book *Educating Anthony*. Some say the sex is hotter, but…you'll have to find out for yourself!

CONNECT WITH KARA ONLINE:

My Website—http://www.Karakeen.com
Facebook—http://facebook.com/karakeenauthor
Twitter—http://twitter.com/karakeenauthor

If you enjoyed reading *Two Much*—please recommend it and review it. If you do review the book on Goodreads or your favorite retailer, feel free to email me and let me know.
KaraKeen.author@gmail.com

www.ingramcontent.com/pod-product-compliance
Lightning Source LLC
Chambersburg PA
CBHW071244130626
46556CB00003B/1152